D1517609

The GUN FIGHT

Richard Matheson

A TOM DOHERTY ASSOCIATES BOOK
NEW YORK

This is a work of fiction. All of the characters, organizations, and events portrayed in this novel are either products of the author's imagination or are used fictitiously.

THE GUN FIGHT

Copyright © 1993 by RXR, Inc.

A Forge Book
Published by Tom Doherty Associates, LLC
175 Fifth Avenue
New York, NY 10010

www.tor-forge.com

Forge® is a registered trademark of Tom Doherty Associates, LLC.

ISBN 978-0-7653-6228-5

First Forge Edition: November 2009

Printed in the United States of America

0 9 8 7 6 5 4 3 2 1

With much gratitude
I dedicate this book to
Gary Goldstein
for giving me a new literary world to explore.

Prologue

He found them on the morning of the fifth day. It had been difficult to track them down. The range was oven-hot from sunup to sundown, the earth so bone dry and hard, it made hoof prints hard to spot. The heat had worn him down. His canteen was almost empty by the time he reached them, his body feeling seared and weak.

The three men were asleep beside a narrow creek, sprawled exhaustedly on their blankets in the shade of a cottonwood tree. He could make out the form of Aaran Graham, the biggest of the three, a tall, bulky man lying on his right side. The other two were younger, slight of build, lying on their backs, Stetsons shading their eyes.

Benton's gaze shifted to their grounded saddles. All six saddlebags bulged with their contents; what the three men had robbed from the Millersview Bank last Thursday afternoon, leaving behind one dead and one badly wounded teller.

Benton drew in a long, tired breath and dismounted slowly. He really *was* getting too old for this kind of thing. Julia had been on his back for months now. Maybe she was right. Maybe it was time to leave the Rangers and settle down. Still, what else did he know how to do?

He slipped the carbine from its scabbard and started down a dusty slope toward the three motionless figures.

He tried to be as quiet as he could but his boots scuffed unavoidably on the hard soil.

He was glancing at the three staked horses when Aaran Graham jerked awake, twisting around, his half-asleep expression one of startled anger.

"Wake up!" he shouted, grabbing for the holstered pistol lying on the ground beside him.

"*Don't do it!*" Benton ordered, snapping up the carbine barrel. He saw the two younger men sitting up groggily.

Graham paid no attention, clutching at the handle of his Colt and starting to raise it.

Benton's shot hit him in the center of the chest, knocking him backward; he was dead before his body hit the ground.

"*Pa!*" The cry of anguish made Benton's gaze jump to the stricken face of one of the younger men.

Before he could react further, the other young man had snatched up his pistol and fired. Benton grunted in surprise as the bullet struck the barrel of his carbine, knocking it from his grip and numbing his fingers.

Training made him dive to his left, avoiding the young man's second shot by less than an inch. As he fell, his right hand dropped to his pistol. It was free of his holster and being fired before the young man could get off another shot.

The bullet slammed into the young man's chest just above the heart and, with a cry of dazed pain, he stumbled back, eyes already glazed over by the death which took him seconds later.

Benton scrambled to his feet, eyes fixed on the remaining young man who, he saw now, was more a boy than a man. He'd had no idea until moments ago that one of Graham's men was his son.

The boy was staring at his dead father, then at the other young man who Benton later learned was his older brother.

Benton was never to forget the expression on the

boy's face. Stunned and horrified, his eyes wide with total disbelief. The look in the boy's eyes was what Benson would remember most; the look of someone whose entire world had just been shattered.

When the boy's hand clawed down for his pistol, Benton stiffened with amazement. "*Don't!*" he cried, unable to believe what he was seeing.

Only habitual reflex kept him alive; an ingrained mechanism that made him fire without thought, hitting the boy in the stomach. He felt a bolt of shock that his aim had been so poor. It had been, he later realized, the measure of his utter dismay that the boy had attempted such a hopeless move.

The boy had stumbled back and sat down heavily on the ground, a blank expression on his face now. He looked down curiously at his stomach, regarding the pump of blood from the bullet hole as though it were coming from someone else.

Then—Benton felt sick to his stomach when he heard it—the boy began to cry.

"Pa," he murmured. "Henry." He repeated the names over and over, sobbing like a frightened child, tears flowing down his cheeks.

Then, finally, before he fainted, he cried out, once, "*It hurts!*"

Benton sank down on the ground, legs suddenly devoid of strength. He looked at Aaran Graham's body. At the body of Henry Graham. Finally, at the thinly breathing form of Graham's younger son; his name was Albert, Benton later discovered. He knew that even if he tried to get the boy back to Millersview, he'd be dead before they were halfway there.

One week later, Benton brought the three bodies back to Millersview after remaining with Albert Graham for the two days it took him to die.

The first thing he did when he got home was go up to the bedroom, open a chest at the foot of the bed, and dump in his pistol, holster, and belt.

When his wife asked him why he'd done that, he told her that he was finished, that he would never wear a pistol as a weapon again.

3:29 P.M., Millersview, Texas, August 13, 1871.

The First Day

Chapter One

The chaparral bird was running a fierce race with the black roan as it pounded across the hard earth. The long legs of the bird flashed wildly in a swirl of alkali dust, ten yards ahead of the roan's battering hooves.

Off the wide trail, a jackrabbit bounded into the brush with great, erratic leaps. Awakened by the muffled thunder in the earth, a coiled rattlesnake writhed sluggishly and lifted its flat head, dead eyes searching.

The tall roan galloped along the trail, its broad legs drawing high, then driving down quickly at the dust-clouded earth. The spur rowels of its young rider raked once across its heaving flanks and the thick weave of muscles underneath its hide drove it on still faster.

Robby Coles paid no attention to the long-beaked roadrunner skittering its weaving path on the trail ahead. He rode close-seated, his knees clamped against the roan's flanks, his booted feet braced forward and out against the stirrups. Beneath the broad brim of his Stetson, his dark eyes peered straight ahead at the out fences of the small ranch he approached.

The driving hooves came too close and the chaparral bird lunged off the trail, racing into the brush. The roan thundered on, following the twists of the trail, a thin froth blowing from its muzzle. Spur rowels scratched again, the horse leaped forward obediently, past the tall and spiny-branched cholla cactus, galloping past the first fence line of the ranch.

Now the rider's eyes focused on the far-off cluster of buildings that comprised the ranch layout. His thin lips pressed together into a blood-pinched line and there was a strained movement in his throat. Was he there? The question drifted like smoke across his mind and he felt sweat dripping down beneath his shirt collar and realized, abruptly, how thirsty he was.

Cold resolve forced itself into his eyes again and his slender hands tightened on the sweat-slick reins. He could feel the rhythmic pounding inside his body as the hooves of his roan pistoned against the hard earth. He could feel the arid bluntness of the wind buffeting across his cheeks and against his forehead; the abrasive rubbing of his legs against the horse's flanks.

There were other things he felt, too.

As the hooves of his mount drummed along the trail, Robby Coles noticed, from the corners of his eyes, the aimless wandering of cattle beyond the fences. He swallowed hot air and coughed once as the dustiness tickled in his throat. The ranch was a half mile distant now. Robby Coles reached down nervously and touched the smooth walnut of his gun stock. He wondered if he should be wearing it.

Merv Linken was coming out of the barn, carrying a pitchfork, when the big black roan came charging into the open area between the barn and the main house.

At first, the horse headed for the main house. Then the rider saw Merv and pulled his mount around sharply. Merv stood watching as the roan cantered over and stopped before him, its flanks heaving, hot breath steaming from its nostrils.

"Hello there, Robby," Merv said, smiling up at the grim-faced young rider. "What brings you out in sech a rush?"

Robby Coles drew in a quick breath and forced it out.

"Benton here?" he asked breathlessly, his dark-eyed gaze drifting toward the main house.

"No, he ain't," Merv said. "Matter o' fact, he's to town gettin' supplies."

He saw how the skin tightened across Robby's cheeks and how his mouth pressed suddenly into a line.

"Guess you rode out fer nothin'," Merv said, then shrugged. "Unless you want to set and wait."

"How long's he been gone?" Robby's voice sounded thin and disturbed above the shuddering pants of his roan. He drew out a bandanna and mopped at his face.

"Oh . . . I reckon, since about eight," Merv said. "Said he was—"

He stopped talking abruptly as Robby jerked the horse around and kicked his spur rowels in. The sweat-flecked roan started forward, breaking into a hard gallop before it passed the bunkhouse.

Merv Linken stood there a while, leaning on the pitchfork, watching Robby Coles ride away toward town. Then he shrugged and turned toward the house.

Julia Benton came walking in quick strides across the yard, drying her hands. She was a tall woman, slender and softly curved, her hair a light blond.

"Who was that?" she asked.

"Young Robby Coles," Merv answered.

"What did he want?"

"Got no notion, ma'm," Merv told her. "Just came in, tight-leggin' and asked for the old man."

"Is that all?"

"That's all, ma'm. Reckon he's headed for Kellville to see Mr. Benton now."

They stood silent for a moment, watching from beneath the shading of their palms, the roan and its rider dwindle into the distance of the brush country.

"He's sure bakin' that hoss," Merv said. "Must be anxious to see yore husband."

Julia Benton stood motionless in the hot sunlight, a look of uneasy curiosity in her eyes. She watched until she couldn't see the horse any longer.

Then she went back to her dishes.

Chapter Two

"**W**ell, I don't know," John Benton said, with a slow shake of his head. "They may scratch Hardin's name from the black book for now." He grinned briefly. "But I think they'll have to put it back in again."

He raked a sulfur match across his boot heel and held the flare to the end of the cigarette he'd just rolled. He grimaced slightly at the acrid sulfur smell in his nostrils, then blew out a puff of smoke from the corner of his mouth. He shook out the match and tossed it into the sand-filled tobacco box on the floor.

"No," he said to the three men at the bar with him. "Writin' off Wes Hardin because he's in Rusk Prison now—that's a bet I wouldn't take."

"You think he'll bust out?" asked Henry Oliver, the portly owner of one of Kellville's dry goods stores.

"Well, I . . . wouldn't think that either," Benton said, picking the cigarette from his lips and blowing out a cloud of smoke. "He'll try bustin' out, sure enough, but that's quite a place to bust out of. I used to go there quite a few times takin' in prisoners." He fingered his glass of whiskey. "Pretty stiff," he said, nodding once. "I wouldn't think he'd bust out."

"How else can he get out then?" Bill Fisher asked him. "He's in for twenty-five years, ain't he?"

Benton thumped down his glass and smacked his lips as the whiskey threaded its heat down his throat.

"Well," he said, "twenty-five years is the sentence, all right. But there's always paroles. Even pardons."

"Damn right," Fisher replied, nodding purse-lipped and staring into the amber depths of his drink. "They's plenty of folks think Wes Hardin got a bum deal for doin' what he had to do. Ain't that right, Benton?"

John Benton twisted his broad-muscled shoulders a little and scratched once at his crop of darkly blond hair.

"Couldn't say, Fisher," he answered, shaking his head. "They never put me on the case. You know as much about Hardin as I do."

"If they *had* put you on the case, John Benton," said Henry Oliver expansively, waving a thick finger at the tall man, "Mister John Wesley Hardin would have been in Rusk Prison long ago."

"He'd a been in the boneyard long ago," John Sutton added hurriedly, his young voice eager to please.

John Benton only chuckled softly and gestured toward Pat, the bartender, for another drink. He put the cigarette between his lips again and listened amusedly as the men went on discussing the imprisonment of Hardin and the possibilities of his escaping. He nodded once to Pat as the glass was filled, then touched the smooth sides of the glass with his long, sure fingers, a mild expression on his strongly cut face.

"Isn't that so, Benton?" said Joe Sutton, with the tone of a novice seeking ultimate authority.

"What's that, Sutton?" Benton asked.

"I say Wes Hardin killed more men with his border roll than any other way."

The beginning of a smile twitched at the corners of Benton's wide mouth. "As I said," he answered, "what I know about Hardin you could put in a pea shell and rattle."

He stiffened suddenly, his legs going rigid, the amiable expression wiped from his face as Joe Sutton reached down for his pistol. Instinctively, his right hand shot across his body to the spot on his left where his pistol would have been if he'd worn one.

Joe Sutton held out his pistol, butt first. "Show how he does it," he asked, oblivious. "Show how Hardin rolls it."

The tenseness melted imperceptibly from Benton's face, his body relaxed and the movement of his hand continued up smoothly to his glass. The smile returned.

"Sutton, never do that," he said, without rancor. "When a man goes for his gun, he should mean business. You can get yourself killed that way."

Sutton looked blank. "Well," he said, "I know you don't pack no gun and I just thought . . ."

His pistol hand dropped and he looked crestfallen. Joe Sutton was one of the many in Kellville who idolized Benton.

"Forget it," Benton said, grinning. "Just don't want to see you leanin' into a bullet. Here, give it here. I'll show you how he does it."

Sutton handed over the pistol happily and Benton opened the cylinder and spilled out six cartridges on the bar top.

He shook his head. "Sutton, you should only put five bullets in the wheel. You keep the hammer on the empty chamber. That's for safety; otherwise you're liable to shoot your leg off."

Sutton looked rueful again. "Think I'll throw it away," he muttered and a chuckle sounded in Benton's deep chest.

"Just have to be careful," he said.

"You want to use my gun too?" Bill Fisher asked. "Hardin uses two."

"One or two, it doesn't matter," Benton said. "Same in either hand."

The three men and the bartender watched in fascination as the tall Benton stepped back from the bar and stuck the pistol under the belt of his Levi's.

"Now say I been throwed down on," he told them. "I didn't get any chance to draw my iron. So the man, whoever he is, asks me to hand over my gun. So . . ."

Benton reached down and the men saw him draw the pistol slowly, then hold it out toward them, butt first, his forefinger curled limply in the trigger guard.

"Then—" Benton said.

Suddenly the pistol blurred in their sight as he rolled it backward and, before they could blink their eyes, the sound of the clicking hammer reached their ears.

"You see, you fire with the webbing of your thumb," Benton told them. "Your trigger finger is just the pivot."

"*Jeez.*" An awed Joe Sutton shook his head slowly. "I couldn't even see it."

Benton smiled. "You're not s'posed to," he said. "That's the point, Sutton." The smile faded. "Anyway it's a snaky trick," he said. "When a man's outdone fair and square, he's got no right to cheat his way back to winning."

In the momentary silence, Joe Sutton asked, "Why don't you pack a gun no more, Benton?"

Benton's almost expressionless gaze flicked up at him.

"Don't ask a man questions like that, Sutton," he said quietly. "That's a man's own business."

"Gee, Benton, I'm sorry. I—" Sutton looked apologetically at him.

But Benton was looking down at the pistol, hefting it idly in his palm as if he were weighing the merits of what it represented to him. For a moment, his mouth was pressed into a firm line. Then he shrugged once.

"Oh, well," he said casually. "Here; catch." He tossed the pistol back to Sutton.

Sutton caught it fumblingly in both hands. Benton tossed his cigarette into the gaboon and shook his head with a wry smile.

"Sutton, you'll have to learn to snatch a gun and set it

goin' at the same time." His eyes glinted with detached amusement. "That is," he said, "if you mean to be a real, sure-fire gun shark."

Sutton still looked blank as Benton took a deep breath and threw off his momentary seriousness.

"Throw it here," he told Sutton. "I'll show you."

Sutton tossed the pistol and saw it plucked cleanly from the air and, in the same moment, fired.

"You see?" Benton said, "there's a lot more to gunplay than just a fast draw."

Without seeming to look, he flung the pistol to his left and cocked and fired it in the second his hand caught it.

"They call it the shift," he said. "You'll need that if your shootin' arm takes a slug."

He tossed the pistol back into his right hand and cocked it, the barrel aimed toward the double doors.

The young man who came pushing through them recoiled with a start, his face paling.

Benton grinned and dropped the pistol barrel. "Don't worry, Coles," he said, "nothin' in the wheel but air."

He tossed the pistol back to Sutton again and returned to his drink as the men greeted Robby.

"What time is it, Pat?" Benton asked the bartender.

Pat drew out his gold watch. "About quarter to eleven," he said.

Benton grunted. "Have to be goin' soon. Or the missus will be riding in after me." His smile was inward, seeming to impart a secret pleasure to him as he picked up his glass.

Then he put down the glass and looked aside.

"You want to see me, Coles?" he asked the young man who stood tensely beside him.

"Yes, I want to see you."

Benton's mouth tightened as he heard the sullen anger in Robby Coles' voice. He took his boot off the rail and turned completely.

"What is it, kid?" he asked curiously.

Robby stood there rigidly, unable to control the shaking in his slender body. At his sides, his hands were clenched into white fists and the repressed fury in his face was thinned by apprehension.

"Well?" Benton asked, his brow furrowing quizzically.

Robby swallowed convulsively.

"You better watch out," he said, hoarsely.

The three men at the bar heard the tenseness in Robby's voice and they looked down curiously at him.

"Watch out for what?" Benton asked.

Robby drew in a ragged breath and let it falter through clenched teeth. "Just be careful," he said, his face growing paler.

Benton's left hand raised up as if in a gesture of question. Then it dropped down and he shook his head in small, tight movement. "I don't get you, kid," he said. "What are you trying to say?"

Robby shuddered and forced his lips together.

"Just leave my girl alone," he said, his voice weakening.

Benton's expression grew suddenly blank. He leaned back as if to get a better look at Robby.

"Your girl?" he said, uncomprehendingly. "What does—"

"Well, she told me!" Robby burst out, suddenly. "So I know, I know! You don't have to lie to me!"

Benton's eyes flinted. "What are you saying?" he asked coldly.

Robby swallowed again, a look of sudden dread flaring in his eyes.

"Let's have it, kid," Benton said. "Chew it finer. What's all this about your girl?"

Robby seemed to dredge down into himself for the strengthening of courage. He drew back his lean shoulders and forced out a rasping breath.

"She told me how you been botherin' her," he said in a clipped voice. "And I'm tellin' you to stop."

The anger drifted from Benton's face. For a long moment, he looked at Robby without expression. Then he shook his head once, as if wonderingly.

"You're out of your mind," he said quietly and turned back to the bar with another shake of his head.

Robby stood there trembling.

"Listen, Benton," he said, the anger desperate in his voice, "I'm not afraid of you."

Benton glanced aside. "Kid," he said, "go home. Get outta here and we'll forget what you said. Just don't hang around."

"Benton, damn it!" Robby yelled.

Benton turned brusquely, his face hard with restrained temper. "Listen, kid, I'm tellin' you to—"

He jerked back his head in sudden shock as the white-faced Robby flailed out with his right fist. Flinging up his left arm, he knocked aside the erratic blow.

"What are you—" he started amazedly, then had to ward aside another blow driven at his chest by Robby. His hand shot down and caught Robby's left wrist in a grip of iron.

"Coles, have you gone plumb—"

But Robby was too far gone now. His lips drawn back in a grimace both furious and terror-stricken, he drove his right fist out again and it thudded off Benton's broad shoulder. The men at the bar watched in dumbfounded amazement and Pat came hurrying around the foot of the counter.

Benton tried to catch Robby's right wrist and pin him completely but, before he could, the bunched fist grazed his left cheek, reddening the skin.

"Well, the hell—" he suddenly snapped and drove a short, pulled blow into Robby's stomach.

Robby doubled over with a breath-sucked grunt and fell against the bar, his mouth jerking open as he tried to catch in the air. Benton hauled him up by the left arm, glancing over at Pat who had just hurried up to them.

"All right?" Pat asked and Benton nodded silently.

"Come here," he told the gagging Robby and tried to lead him to one of the tables.

Robby tore away with a whining gasp, then started to buckle and Benton caught him again.

"Come over here with me," he said, the anger gone from his voice. "Let's get this figured."

Again Robby tore away with a sob and backed off, forcing himself to an erect position, hands pressed to his stomach.

"Damn you," he gasped through shaking, blood-drained lips. "I'll get you, Benton, I swear I'll get you."

Benton stood there silently, hands hanging loosely at his sides as Robby turned and staggered down the length of the saloon floor and shoved through the double doors.

After a moment, he shook his head in slow wonder.

"I'll be damned," he said and looked over at the staring men. "I will be damned," he muttered to himself and returned to his still unfinished drink.

"What was on *his* mind?" Pat asked, behind the bar again.

"You got me," Benton said. "It's over my head, *way* over."

Pat grunted and wiped idly at the dark, glossy wood of the bar counter. Down the way, Bill Fisher and Henry Oliver exchanged glances.

"Who is his girl, anyway?" Benton asked curiously.

Pat shrugged. "Got no notion," he said. "Some town girl, I reckon."

Benton made an amused sound and shook his head. "Bothered her," he said. "I don't even know who she is."

"Louisa Harper, that's his girl," Joe Sutton said quickly and the two men, glancing aside, saw that Sutton had edged along the bar in order to join their conversation. Benton's mouth tightened a little but he didn't say anything.

"Her mother's the Widow Harper," Sutton hurried on, oblivious. "Aunt runs a lady clothes store cross the square."

Benton and Pat exchanged a glance and the corners of Benton's mouth twitched, repressing a wry smile. Down the bar, Henry Oliver stretched and told Bill Fisher that he intended going over to Jesse Willmark's Barber Shop for a haircut.

Benton heard him and nodded to himself. "Oh, that's right," he said. "I keep meanin' to get a haircut myself. Missus Benton keeps askin' me and it keeps slippin' my mind." He picked up his glass and emptied it.

"You want me to find out about Robby Coles?" Sutton asked abruptly. "You want me to check for you, Benton?"

Benton looked aside, patiently.

"Listen, kid," he said quietly, "just leave it set, hear? Just forget it."

Sutton looked down gloomily into his drink. "Just wanted to help you," he said.

"Well, you gotta learn the difference between helpin' and stickin' your nose in where it don't belong, kid," Benton told him, without rancor.

Sutton's expression was dully morose. "Didn't *mean* nothin'," he muttered.

Benton clapped the young man on the shoulder once with his broad palm. "Okay, kid, let's forget it. No hard feelin's." He put his Stetson on, then dug into his Levi's pocket for silver.

"Well, I have to drag it," he said. "Lots o' work to do."

The three men at the bar were silent as Benton walked in long, unhurried strides for the doors. They were still silent as he went out. It was only after they heard the sound of his buckboard rolling away from the saloon hitching rack that they turned to each other and started talking.

Chapter Three

Jesse Willmark was sitting in one of his two barber chairs, reading the *Kellville Weekly Bugle*. It was quiet in the small shop, so quiet that the sluggish drone of fat flies could be clearly heard. The only other sound was that of Jesse turning the newspaper pages with idle fingers, his heavyset body slumped lethargically on the black leather cushion.

The wall clock struck eleven with a tinny resonance. Jesse reached into his pocket and checked his watch. He shook his head disgustedly. The wall clock was ten minutes slow again and he'd just had it repaired three years before.

The click of heels near the door made Jesse look up quickly. "*Oh.*" His head dipped once in a nod and he smiled as he pushed up.

"Howdy, Mr. Oliver," he said and slid quickly from the chair, tossing the newspaper onto one of the wire-backed chairs along the wall. "Set you down and we'll get right to it."

Henry Oliver slid out of his waistcoat and hung it carefully on the clothes tree beside his hat. Then, he settled back in the ornate barber chair with a sigh and shifted himself into a comfortable position as Jesse fastened the big cloth around his thick neck.

"Nice day, today," Jesse said automatically and Henry

Oliver mumbled an assent as Jesse picked up the scissors, clicked the blades together his habitual four times, and began cutting.

"Funny thing at the Zorilla Saloon before," Henry Oliver said after a few moments of idle conversation had passed.

"Oh?" Jesse said, eyebrows raising in practiced fashion. "What's that, Mr. Oliver?"

"You know young Robby Coles," Oliver said and Jesse said, "Mmm-hmm," cutting and clipping. "Know his father well. Fine man, fine man."

"Yes. Well . . ." said Henry Oliver, "the boy came charging into the saloon and started a fight. With John Benton."

Jesse's mouth gaped for a moment. "*No*," he said. "*John Benton*? Well, I'll be . . ."

"Yup." Henry Oliver's head nodded vigorously and Jesse held back the scissors until the nodding stopped. "Quite a fight, *quite a fight.* Benton won, of course. Doubled young Robby over with a gut punch."

"No," Jesse said incredulously, snipping and running the comb teeth through his customer's graying hair. "John Benton. Well. What were they fightin' over?"

Henry Oliver crossed his dark-trousered legs. "That's what I don't figure," he said, vaguely mysterious. "The boy accused Benton of—" He looked around carefully. "Of playing around with his girl."

"No! You me—" Jesse's voice broke off, startledly. "Louisa Harper? Playin' around?" His voice rose and fell in jagged peaks and valleys of expression. "I can't believe it," he said, shaking his head. "Strangest thing I ever heard. John Benton. Huh." His nervous right hand clicked the scissor blades in the air and he went on cutting. "Be damned," he said.

"Well you could have knocked me down with your finger," Henry Oliver said. "Surprised the life out of me, naturally."

"Well, naturally," Jesse said, shaking his head, an intent look on his thick-featured face.

"And I wasn't the only one there," said Henry Oliver. "Bill Fisher was there. And young Joe Sutton. And Pat heard too, yes, Pat heard it all. Strange, all right."

Jesse kept shaking his head. "You . . . think it's true?" he asked.

"Well . . ." Henry Oliver's brow tightened. "I couldn't say," he ventured solemnly. "Offhand, I'd say no but . . . well, you can't tell, you just can't tell about those things. I know I wouldn't want to be the one to start a story like that. John Benton's too big a man around here to . . ." His voice drifted off and the shop was still except for the clicking scissor blades.

"Yes, he's admired, all right," Jesse said then as if there had been no lapse in the conversation. "Always thought he's been overrated but . . . well, that's nothing to do with this." He shook his head, cutting absorbedly. "Louisa Harper, huh?" he said. "Now ain't that somethin'."

"Oh," Henry Oliver said, almost grudgingly, his thick shoulders shrugging slightly, "it might be a mistake, of course."

"Sure. Sure, that's right, it could be a mistake," Jesse said, agreeing with a customer.

Twenty minutes later, Henry Oliver walked out of the shop and Jesse sat down again to look at his paper. But he didn't read it, he just sat there staring at the blurred print and thinking about what Mr. Oliver had said.

"Sure," he muttered to himself. "Sure. I can see it; him a hero and all." He licked his fat lips. "Louisa Harper, huh? I wouldn't mind—"

He broke off abruptly as another customer entered. There was the taking off of the coat, the sitting down in the gilded metal and black leather chair, the tying of the cloth, the comment on the weather, the assent, the plucking up of the long scissors, the tentative clicking of blades.

"Heard about the big fight?" Jesse asked his customer.

"No. When was this?" the man asked casually.

"Just a while ago," said Jesse. "In the Zorilla Saloon. Robby Coles and John Benton."

"No." The man looked up interestedly. "Benton?"

"Yup." Jesse's head nodded in short, decisive arcs as he worked, purse-lipped, on the man's hair. "Had a fight over Robby Cole's girl, Louisa Harper."

"You don't tell me," the man said, face strained with interest.

"That's right," Jesse said calmly. "That's right." His small eyes narrowed. "'Course it might be a mistake but it *seems* . . . there's been somethin' between Benton and the girl."

The customer's eyes rose to the mirror on the wall and he and Jesse looked at each other with the half-repressed fascination of little boys who believe they have unearthed something of unique prurience.

"*Well*," the man said.

As they went on talking, the sound of their conversation drifted out the door into the air of Kellville.

Chapter Four

Matthew Coles was never on any horse but his chestnut gelding. He did not ride well and was a man who would not let himself be observed doing anything less than perfectly. The chestnut was a mild animal, easily seated, but one which managed to give the appearance of being excitably alert. It was a combination well suited to Matthew Coles who preferred his triumphs to appear hard-won. Thus, satisfyingly, was the gelding added to his list of conquests, which list included also his acquaintances, business associates, wife, and children. Matthew Coles was a man who kept a taut, unyielding rein on every aspect of his life.

It was just ten minutes past noon when he came riding slowly down Armitas Street. At the twelfth stroke of noon, he had risen from the bench of his gunsmith shop, donned his coat and hat, and locked up the shop, leaving in the door window the thumb-worn sign which read simply DINNER. He had mounted the docile chestnut and started for his house where, by God, Jane had better have dinner immediately ready to eat. Precision and efficiency—Matthew Coles was especially guided by these coupled verities.

Mr. Coles was in a particularly sour humor that afternoon. His elder son, Robby, had not appeared at the shop promptly at eight thirty as he was supposed to; as a matter of fact, Robby had not shown up at all. That was an added reason why Matthew Coles rode stiffly, his back a ramrod of irked authority, his face set with dominance defied. He wore black, as always, for it made his five foot ten inches appear taller and, he fancied, made him look unusually handsome for a man in his middle fifties.

As he rode into the alleyway beside the house, he saw his son's roan tied up in back and his mouth twitched angrily. The horse hadn't been rubbed down, it was streaked over with dry sweat. Beneath taut lips, Matthew Coles' false teeth clamped vice-like. Fool!—he raged within. Robby didn't deserve a horse and, by God, if he didn't take better care of it, he wouldn't *have* a horse!

The gelding stopped. Matthew Coles eased his right leg over its croup and let himself down with a grunt. Then he led the horse into the small stable and tied it up near the water trough.

He crossed the backyard with vengeful strides, then clumped loudly up the wooden porch steps, removing his hat as he ascended.

The kitchen door thudded shut behind him and his wife Jane straightened up over the chair in which Robby sat slumped.

"Good afternoon, dear," she said hastily. "I'll get you your—"

"What is the meaning of leaving your mount untended?" Coles asked loudly, ignoring his mouse-haired wife.

Robby looked up, his drained features tensed with nausea. "I was sick," he muttered. "I—"

"Speak up, sir. I can't hear you when you mumble like a child." Mr. Coles hung up his hat with one authoritative motion.

Robby swallowed, grimacing with pain, his hands pressed over the waist of his belt-loosened trousers.

"Matthew, he's ill."

Matthew Coles impaled his small-framed wife with an imperious glare. "Is my dinner ready?" he challenged.

"I was—"

"I've been working," her husband explained with the carefully measured articulation of a harried father addressing his idiot daughter. "I'm hungry. Are you going to stand there gaping at me or are you going to make my dinner?"

Mrs. Coles tried to look agreeable but could not summon the long-lost ability to smile. She turned away and hurried toward the stove.

"Well, sir?" Mr. Coles re-addressed his bent-over son.

"I'm sorry, sir," Robby said, his lips drawn back from his teeth. He groaned slightly and, by the stove, his mother cast a look of anguished concern toward him.

"What's wrong with you, sir?" Matthew Coles demanded. "And where were you this entire morning?"

"I was—" Robby leaned over suddenly, jamming the end of one fist against his pale-lipped mouth.

"Matthew, he's ill," Mrs. Coles said suddenly. "Please don't—"

"This is not your discussion," her husband informed her, face tensed with the expression of a soldier attacked on all sides. "I have an appointment at the bank at one o'clock. I expect to be there exactly on time—fed."

Jane Coles' hands twitched in futile empathy with her upset condition and she turned back to the stove, a hopeless expression on her face.

"Where is the boy?" her husband asked her.

"He's not home from school yet," she answered.

"I can't hear you."

"I say, he's not home from school yet."

"He's *supposed* to be home. I think a little strapping is in order for that young man."

His wife said nothing, knowing that no answer was expected. She went about quietly at her work as Matthew Coles concentrated on Robby again.

"Why weren't you at your work this morning?"

Robby looked up at his stern-faced father with pain-glossed eyes.

"Sir, I expect an answer."

"I went out," Robby said, weakly.

"Out? Out where?"

"T-to . . . John Benton's . . . ranch."

"And what, may I ask, were you doing there?"

"I . . ." Robby swallowed and gasped in air. "I wanted to see . . . to see him."

"About what?"

Robby stared at his father, his lean chest rising and falling with tight, spasmodic movements.

"I am waiting, sir," his father said clearly.

"I . . . sir, I'd rather not—"

"*What was that?*" His father spoke the words in a cold, threatening tone and spots of color flared up in Robby's pale cheeks. His throat moved again as he looked up fearfully into the hard face of his father.

Robby bit his lip. "I had to see B-Benton," he said.

"What about?" Matthew Coles spoke the words slowly, with the repetitious demanding of a man who would not be put off.

Robby looked down at his boots. "Lou-Louisa," he said.

"Miss Louisa Harper?" asked his father, announcing her name as if it were the title of a book.

Robby nodded slowly without looking up.

"And what about Miss Louisa Harper?"

"I . . ."

"Answer me this moment, sir!"

Robby looked up in hopeless despair. "I wanted to f-find out about her and . . . and Benton."

At the stove the father and son heard Mrs. Coles catch her breath. "Robby," she murmured faintly.

Matthew Coles paid no attention. His face a block of carved stone, he caught at the situation as one worthy of his stern attention.

"Make yourself clear, sir," he said firmly and distinctly.

Robby's throat moved convulsively as he stared up.

"Well?"

"Louisa told me that . . . that Benton annoyed her and . . . tried to . . . to—"

"*To effect a meeting?*" His father completed the sentence with imperial outrage, his nostrils flared, his hands clenched suddenly at his sides.

Robby's head slumped forward and a harsh breath shuddered his body. "I guess," he muttered.

Mr. Coles drew back his shoulders slowly as if he were getting ready to gird his loins for a battle with all the forces of evil in the world.

"You saw Benton," he said and it wasn't a question.

Robby nodded. "I . . . yes, I . . . did."

"And what was his defense?"

"He . . . he acted like he didn't kn-know anything about it."

A thin, humorless smile raised the ends of Matthew Coles' lips. "Of course," he said quietly, "that would be what he'd say." He looked down dispassionately at his son's pain-tightened face. "There was a fight," he stated.

Robby nodded and mumbled something.

Then Matthew Coles was leaning over his son and Mrs. Coles was watching her husband with uneasy eyes.

"Miss Harper is your intended bride, is she not?" said Matthew Coles, his voice calm.

Robby looked up quickly at his father and nodded. "Y . . . yes," he said, almost tentatively, as if he suspected that his father was going to throw the admission back in his face.

"Well, then," Mr. Coles said, still calmly, as he straightened up. "What do you mean to do about it?"

In the sudden silence of the kitchen, Robby distinctly heard the frightened sound his mother made. But there seemed nothing visible in the entire room except his black-suited father looking down commandingly at him.

Chapter Five

A little after twelve, the spotted hound raced to the Dutch door and reared up excitedly, its blunt claws scratching at the wood, its hoarse barking echoing in the kitchen. Julia Benton looked up from her pea shelling with a quick smile that drove the tense absorption from her face.

Five minutes later the buckboard came creaking across the yard and braked up in back of the house.

Julia walked over to the door and opened the top half. She saw her tall husband reaching over the iron railing for one of the baskets in the buckboard. "*Hush* now," she told the baying hound.

"Hello, ma," John said, grinning as he came struggling toward the door with his heavy load.

"Hello, dear." Julia pulled open the bottom half of the door and the wriggling hound rushed out, its long tail blade whipping at its flanks. "Howdy, mutt," Benton said as he entered the kitchen, heeled by the excited dog.

Benton set the basket down heavily on the table and straightened up with a quickly exhaled breath. "Am I late?" he said.

Julia nodded, smiling. "The boys finished half hour ago. Sit down and I'll warm you what's left."

"Right. I'll get the rest of the chuck first, though."

Benton left the kitchen, the dog prancing and growling happily at his boots. "Easy there, Jughead," Julia heard her husband tell the hound.

A minute later, Benton sat at the table, checking the supply list while Julia warmed his dinner.

"Twenty pounds Arbuckle's," he said, laying down the coffee sack. "Canned cow. Salt. Flour."

"Molasses?" she said.

He nodded with a grunt. "Yup," he said, "black strap." He checked off the item. "Oh, I forgot," he said, "I got you canned peaches. Maxwell just got some in from the east."

"*Oh*," she said, happily surprised, "that's nice. We'll have them Sunday morning."

Benton smiled to himself and worked on the list until Julia put his dinner on the table. Then he washed up and sat down. By the stove, the hound was going back to twitching sleep again.

"John?" Julia asked him while he ate.

"What?"

"What did Robby Coles want to see you about?"

He looked up from his plate in surprise. "How did you know about that?" he asked.

"He rode here first looking for you."

"He did, eh?" Benton sipped a little hot coffee from the mug. "Well, I'll be," he said, shaking his head.

"You saw him in town then," she said.

Benton nodded. "Yeah. Funny thing too," he said. "He was all horns and rattles. Came into the Zorilla Saloon and threw a fist at me."

She stood by the table looking concerned. "But why?" she asked.

He shrugged, food in his mouth, then swallowed. "I don't know," he said. "That's the part that don't make sense. He told me to stop botherin' his girl."

She looked at him silently a moment. "His *girl*?" she said.

"That's right. Came up to me blowin' a storm and

tells me to leave his girl alone. Then he throws a punch at me. What do you think o' that?"

Julia shook her head slowly. "But . . . why should he say such a thing to you?" she asked.

"Don't ask me, ma. I didn't even know who the girl was until the Sutton kid told me."

"Who is she?"

"Louisa Harper, Sutton said. Who's she?"

"Louisa Harper." Julia put two fingers against her cheek and stared into space, trying to place the name. "I don't think I ever—"

Suddenly her mouth opened a second in surprised realization. "I think I know," she said.

"What?" he said, still eating.

"You know the girl I keep telling you about; the one who stares at you in church?"

"You *tell* me there's a girl who stares. I never saw one."

"Oh, you wouldn't notice," she said with the affectionate scorn of a wife. "But she does stare at you. And . . . yes, come to think of it," she went on, nodding to herself, "I think I've seen her walking with Robby Coles after church."

"So," he said. "Any more coffee?"

She poured the heavy black coffee into his mug. "You know what I think?" she asked him.

"What's that?"

"I think she told Robby Coles that you pestered her."

"That's right, that's what I said," he answered, nodding. "That's what Coles *told* me she said."

"Well, of course," she said.

Benton looked up at his pretty wife with a grin. "Of course *what*, ma?" he asked.

"Louisa Harper is in love with you."

He stared at her, speechless. "She—"

"In love with you." Julia nodded with a confident smile. "Of course she is. All the girls in Kellville are in love with you. You're their big hero."

"Oh . . ." Benton waved a disgusted hand, ". . . that's hogwash."

She smiled at him.

"That's nonsense, Julia," he insisted.

"No, it isn't," she said with a laugh. "Ever since we moved here everyone's looked up to you. The boys look at you as if you were a god. The girls look at you as if—"

"Why should they?" John said, embarrassed.

"Because you're a hero to them, dear," she said. "You're John Benton, the fearless Ranger, the quick-shooting lawman."

He peered at her until the mock-serious expression on her face broke into an impish grin. "Ha, ha," he said flatly.

"It's true," she said. "To them you're Hardin and Longley and . . . and Hickok all rolled into one."

"That's nonsense," he said. "I haven't worn a gun in town the whole two years we've been here."

"Yes, but they know what you did in the Rangers."

"Oh, that's silly," he mumbled and reached for his coffee mug.

She sat down with her peas again. "Yes, I expect that's what it is," she said. "She's in love with you and she probably dreamed out loud in front of Robby."

"Well, that's stupid," he said in disgust. "If it's true, that is. What's the matter with the girl, doesn't she know any better than that? She has that Coles kid thinkin' I'm a . . . a gallivantin' dude or somethin'."

Julia laughed. "He'll get over it," she said, "as soon as he knows it isn't true."

"How do you know it isn't true?" Benton said, forcing down the grin with effort.

Julia looked up at her husband with soft eyes for a moment, then back to her moving fingers.

"I know," she said, gently.

Chapter Six

Agatha Winston walked down Davis Street in the late afternoon, her thin legs whipping like reeds against the heavy blackness of her skirt and the half dozen petticoats beneath. She was a tall, gaunt woman with eyes of jade, and features molded in sharp angles and pinches. She was a hidebound churchgoer who used her self-styled Christianity as a bludgeon on all those not in the accredited fold.

Right now Agatha Winston was on a crusade.

Like a dark bird of vengeance, she swooped down on the small house of her sister, umbrella stem clicking on the plank sidewalk, skirts a vindictive rustle. Mouth a gash, she shoved in the gate and kicked it shut behind her as she clumped and swished toward the porch steps.

Inside the house, the bell tinkled reactively to the wrathful tugging of Agatha Winston's clawlike fingers. She stood tensely before the door, one black and pointed shoe-tip tapping steadily at the porch, the other pressing down a corner of the welcome mat.

There was a stirring in the house. From its depths, Miss Winston heard the voice of her sister calling, "I'll be right there," and then the light sound of her sister's shoes across an inside floor. Through the gauzy haze of freshly laundered curtains, Miss Winston saw her sister's approach.

The door opened. "Agatha," said the widow Harper in surprise.

"Elizabeth," Miss Winston replied with a concise moving of lips.

"Come in, my dear, please," Elizabeth Harper said, stepping aside, her soft, pink face wrinkled in a welcoming smile. "My, what a lovely surprise."

"That's as it may be," declared Agatha Winston. "You may not think so when you find out why I'm here."

The widow Harper looked confused as she shut the door quietly, then turned back to her sister who was driving her black umbrella into the stand like a mariner harpooning a whale. She stood smiling pleasantly while Agatha removed her bonnet with quick, agitated motions.

Agatha Winston lifted a piercing glance up the stairwell. "Where is Louisa?" she asked in a guarded tone.

"Why . . . up in her room, Agatha," Elizabeth Harper said, looking curiously at her sister. "Why do you—"

Miss Winston took her sister's arm with firm fingers and led her into the quiet, sun-flecked sitting room.

"Sit down," she said curtly and the widow Harper settled like a diffident butterfly on the couch edge, one hand plucking at the grey-threaded auburn of her curls. She was forty-four, a gentle woman, helpless in all things.

Agatha Winston looked down grimly at the rose-petal cheeks of her sister.

"I don't suppose you've heard," she said.

"Heard?" The widow Harper swallowed nervously. She had always been somewhat afraid of her elder sister.

"It's shocking," Miss Winston said in sudden anger. "It's just shocking."

Elizabeth Harper looked dismayed. Her hands stirred restlessly in the lap of her yellow patterned calico, then twined frail fingers.

"What . . . is, Agatha?" she asked, uneasily.

"The terrible gossip that's going around town," Agatha Winston said. "The shameful story . . . about Louisa."

Alarm flared up suddenly in the widow Harper's face as she heard mentioned her only child. "Louisa?" she said hastily. "What about her, Agatha?"

Agatha Winston sat down on the couch with one sure motion, legs and back making a perfect right angle, face stern with righteous indignation.

"She's told you nothing?" she asked her sister.

The widow Harper's lower lip trembled. "Told me about what?" she asked, eyes almost frantic.

Miss Winston drew in a harsh breath. "I think we had better ask Louisa about that," she said. "I don't even want to speak of it until I hear what she has to say." She stood, a bleak wraith of resolution. "Come," she said.

Elizabeth Harper fluttered up. "Agatha, *please*. What *is* it?" she begged.

Agatha Winston clasped gaunt hands before her breast.

"What do you know of Mister John Benton?" she asked bluntly.

Her sister stared back without comprehension. "John Benton?" she repeated the name. "What—"

"Early this afternoon—about two o'clock I'll allow—Mrs. Van Dekker came into the shop." Agatha Winston's dark eyes probed at her sister's. "She told me something that made me shudder . . . positively shudder, Elizabeth."

Elizabeth Harper pressed trembling fingers to her lips and stared fearfully at her sister.

"I won't go into detail," Miss Winston said firmly. "The story may not even be true—I pray to heaven it

isn't—but it concerns this John Benton and . . ." Her
lips pressed together. ". . . *Louisa*," she finished.

Louisa Harper was dreaming. Across the lilac spread of
her bed, her sixteen-year-old body lay, stomach down,
chin propped up by delicately cupped hands. Her blue
eyes stared vacantly out of the window. She was taking
that ride again.

She had taken it a hundred times, maybe more. It was
almost always the same. The petty details of its genesis
were ignored. That she could not ride and was frightened to death of horses mattered little. She was out on
the range again, riding, her light chestnut hair flowing in
the wind, her firm body jolting with the cantering gait
of the horse. The sun was bright—for now.

Then the complication, the always occurring complication. Louisa Harper's lips stirred, her mind stared
deeper into her dream.

A rattlesnake, a road runner, a jackrabbit—the actual
cause was not important. All that mattered was the result;
her horse shying, rearing up with a head-jerking whinny,
then breaking into a frightened gallop across the brush
country. Her scream of terror pulsing in the hot air . . .

. . . and heard.

Her body squirmed a little, her stomach pressing
slightly at the bedspread. A movement at her smooth
throat. The horse galloping, galloping, her holding on
with desperate fear, screaming and hysterical.

Then, out of the mist of her dream, the horseman
riding, tall and erect in the saddle, his clothes dark, his
hat hanging off his shoulders by its bonnet strings, his
blond hair ruffling in the high wind. Closer and closer,
the horseman coming, handsome face resolute, one
strong hand on the reins, the other half raised toward
her . . .

She kept the scene alive; it fascinated her with its terrible thunder of hooves, its pulse-quickening suspense—
with the inevitability of its delicious conclusion.

Which came in a sudden command of her will. Her breath caught, her hands were numb. She felt herself swept off the bolting mount and pulled harshly against the tall rider. The horse reined up and, there they were, alone in the vast, empty range, close together on the tall man's horse.

Oh, Mr. Benton, thank you for saving me.

His eyes gentle on her, his strong arm seeming to tighten around her slender waist. Or was that imagination?

My pleasure, Miss Harper, he said. She felt the butt of his pistol pressing at her hip and it made her shiver.

The scene running, coagulating, breaking again into clarity. Sunlight driven from the sky by needs of plot, deepening shadows over the earth, gray menace swirling in the sky.

Oh, it's going to rain, Mister Benton. We'll get soaked.
I know a place where we can wait out the storm.

Rain failing, a sudden desired squall of it. A small cave in the hills, far from town. But they didn't reach the cave in time and both of them were soaked. Louisa stood by the abruptly built fire, blouse clinging wetly to her swelling form. *I don't care if he sees, I don't.*

You'd better take off those clothes, Miss Harper.
Why, Mr. Benton.

That smile, that throat-catching smile. *I'll look the other way. We have to get our clothes off though or we'll catch our death of cold.*

Scene changing, blurring, transition uncertain, unclear—but definite. Her in her shift, a blanket across her smooth white shoulders. Him with his shirt off; her eyes stealing across the hard-muscled bronze of his torso.

Listen to the wind. His deep, his wonderful voice. *Looks like we may be caught here quite a spell.*

I don't care.

The sudden look exchanged; beneath the blanket, her

small hands trembling. I said it to him and I'd say it again.

Coffee, somehow made, the two of them drinking it in the warm cave, looking into the orange flicker of the fire, the sparks like fireflies darting up into the darkness. The hot trickle of coffee in her throat; suspense. Her young body writhed a little on the bed, throat dry, mouth dry.

The blanket slipping off one shoulder; her leaving it that way. Let him see me, I don't care. His eyes glowing in the firelight, the rain pouring and rushing outside in the black night. His hands reaching.

Sudden wild excitement *Oh, John, John!* . . .

"Louisa?"

She started sharply on the bed at the sound of her mother's frail voice in the hallway. At once, her delicate features twisted into angry lines. The cave scene went funneling down into the bottomless well of thought and Louisa looked at the door with fierce resentment.

"What *is* it?" she asked.

"May we come in, dear?"

One small fist beat down angrily on the bedspread. Louisa rolled over and sat up, her legs dropping over the edge of the mattress. She swallowed heavily, her mouth feeling feather-dry. *We?* she thought.

"Come in," she said sullenly, glancing down at herself. As the knob turned, she ran smoothing fingers over the wrinkles of her skirt.

The two women entered.

"Aunt Agatha," Louisa said, feeling a sudden dropping sensation in her stomach at the appearance of her aunt.

Agatha Winston nodded brusquely at her pretty niece, then, when her sister failed to do so, she shut the door firmly as though to close away all intruding eyes. Louisa glanced covertly at her aunt while the widow Harper came over to the bed, an uncertain smile on her face.

"What is it, mother?" Louisa asked, her eyes lowering now to avoid the gaze of her turning aunt.

"Well, dear, we—"

"We want to speak to you, Louisa," Agatha Winston said, assuming, as her natural due, the role of inquisitor.

That sinking in her stomach again. "Talk to me?" asked Louisa faintly, trying hard to remember if she'd done anything to offend her aunt. Was she supposed to have come to the shop today? No, it couldn't be that; she only worked there Mondays, Wednesdays, and Fridays in return for the financial aid Aunt Agatha gave to them.

The bed creaked as Louisa's mother sat down gingerly beside her. Louisa glanced at her with the effort of a smile trying her lips. "What is it, mother?" she asked.

Her mother smiled nervously, then glanced toward Agatha for help.

"Louisa," said her aunt.

"Yes, Aunt Agatha."

"I am going to ask you a question to which I expect an honest answer." Agatha Winston leaned forward, her beak-like nose aiming at Louisa like a spear point, her black eyes searching. "Remember, Louisa," she cautioned, "there's nothing to be afraid of as long as you tell the truth."

"Darling," murmured Elizabeth Harper, covering one of her daughter's hands with her trembling own. Louisa glanced nervously at her mother, then back again to her aunt. She didn't understand.

Aunt Agatha said, "What has John Benton to do with you?"

Louisa couldn't stop the catching of breath in her throat, the paling of cheek, the startled widening of her eyes.

"John Ben—" she began, then stopped, her voice failing. She felt her heart beating heavily and had the pointed sensation of her mind being ripped open, her most secret thoughts plucked out, naked and terrible. For a second she thought she might faint so strong was the welling of shock.

Agatha Winston straightened up with a look of vulpine self-justification on her lean face. She glanced once at the lined face of her sister, then back to Louisa whose cheeks were now coloring embarrassedly.

"W-why do you ask that, Aunt . . ." Louisa swallowed hastily, ". . . Agatha?" she finished.

"What has John Benton to do with you?"

"N-nothing, Aunt Agatha. I don't even—"

"*Louisa.*" Aunt Agatha's voice threatened and Louisa stopped talking. "You have nothing to be afraid of as long as you tell the truth like the good Christian girl I hope you are."

Numbly, Louisa felt her aunt's gaunt hand fall on her shoulder.

"But—" she began.

"We expect the truth, Louisa," her aunt said.

Louisa stopped again and sat there, heart pulsing heavily in her chest.

"There was a fight this morning, Louisa," Agatha Winston said. "Between John Benton and the young man you will probably marry."

"Rob—" Louisa's voice broke off and she stared up speechlessly at the hard face of her aunt. She wanted to run from the room; go anywhere to get away from her aunt. Her throat moved in a convulsive swallow. I didn't mean it, the thought wavered across her mind, I didn't mean it at all . . .

"The facts are not clear," Aunt Agatha said in concise tones, "but it appears that young Coles was defending your honor against that . . . *man.*"

Louisa felt herself drawing in, backed into a defenseless corner. How could this have happened? She'd had no idea Robby would take her joking taunt so seriously. She'd only wanted to make him angry and jealous and put some life into him.

"Darling, what did that terrible man do to you?" Elizabeth Harper asked in a faint voice, fearing the worst.

"Mother, I don't—"

"Before we go any further, Louisa," her aunt said crisply, "I want you to know that this is a very serious matter. We must have the truth. If you lie, you will be severely punished, do you understand?" She ignored the startled look on her sister's face. "This is a matter of grave importance to your very future."

Louisa looked at her aunt with frightened eyes. It wasn't a lie, her mind struggled to explain. It was only a joke, I only wanted to make him jealous. But she knew her aunt wouldn't see it that way. I didn't mean anything, she thought in anguish.

"*Did* John Benton attempt to arrange an immoral meeting with you?" Agatha Winston demanded bluntly.

Louisa pressed trembling fingers to her lips, her eyes stark with fright. "No," she murmured. "No, he—"

"Don't *lie* to us, Louisa!"

Louisa began sobbing. She felt warm tears falling across her cheeks as she sat there, shaking without control, hardly feeling the pressure of her mother's arm around her back, hardly hearing the frail voice trying to comfort her. Through the blurring prisms of her tears, Louisa saw the shapeless black form of her aunt standing over her. She wanted to tell the truth. She wanted to tell them that she'd only made it up but she was afraid of her aunt, she didn't want to be punished for lying. She was afraid of being scorned, terror-stricken at the thought of anyone knowing her secret. . . .

"When did this happen?" Agatha's voice came breaking down over her like a spray of ice.

"I don't know, I d-don't know!" Louisa sobbed and the widow Harper looked up imploringly at her sister.

"Please, Agatha," she begged, "no more. She's too upset."

"We must know the facts."

"It's not important!" Louisa blurted out suddenly,

her voice rising brokenly. "It isn't important, Aunt Agatha!"

"It is *very* important," the answer came sternly. "Your honor is the most important thing in your life."

"But I didn't—" Fear broke off Louisa's words again and she slumped over, shoulders trembling helplessly.

"No, you didn't tell us immediately," Agatha interpreted her niece's unfinished sentence. "You told Robby Coles and he did what he had to do; went up against that . . . that *killer* to defend your honor. You should be grateful that your honor is so highly regarded."

"Agatha, please," begged her sister.

"Come, Elizabeth."

"I'd like to stay with her, Agatha, and . . ."

She stopped as Agatha's bony hand closed over her shoulder firmly. Agatha shook her head. "Come," she said again and Elizabeth was drawn up nervously, one shaking hand patting at Louisa's soft hair.

"Darling, don't fret now," her mother tried to comfort Louisa. "It isn't your fault, mother knows that."

"Elizabeth," Agatha said strongly, then looked down at her sobbing niece. "You had better remain in the house the rest of the day," she said. "I'll see you at the shop tomorrow morning."

Louisa raised her tear-streaked face quickly as though to speak. Then she sat staring wordlessly at her aunt. I didn't *mean* it, her mind implored but she couldn't speak the words aloud. She was too afraid of her aunt and of the punishment she would get for lying and causing Robby Coles to fight in her defense. In her mind she could almost hear the questions her Aunt Agatha would ask if she confessed. Why did you make up such a story? Why John Benton? Are you trying to say you care for that man?

No, she couldn't bear that, she *couldn't*. She sat silently as the two women moved for the door. Then the door edge had shut off the worried face of her mother and she was alone in the quiet of the room, a sense of impending dread creeping over her.

I didn't mean it, I didn't—she thought again. She'd only told Robby what she did in order to make him jealous. She'd never even dreamed that he'd take it so seriously, that he'd go looking for Benton to fight him. Robby just wasn't that kind; he was the quiet, dull kind, not at all like John Benton.

Louisa Harper sat on the edge of the bed, her sobs gradually subsiding, her breathing getting more and more even. She rubbed at the tears with shaking fingers, then stood and got a handkerchief from her bureau drawer.

She sat on the bed again, looking down at the hooked rug her mother had made for her sixteenth birthday.

Now that Aunt Agatha was out of the room, the situation didn't seem so bad. She knew she really should have told the truth but there was something about her aunt that terrified. She just didn't dare tell that she'd made up the story; especially now after she'd failed to confess it when she'd had the opportunity.

Besides—her right foot began kicking a little, thumping back against the bed—besides, it would all blow over. It wasn't *that* serious, no matter what Aunt Agatha said. Robby wouldn't go any further and certainly John Benton wouldn't; *he* was a gentleman.

The hint of a smile played on Louisa Harper's full lips and something stirred in her. There was something strangely exciting about the thought of John Benton fighting over her.

Louisa shuddered, lips parted suddenly.

The two women stood in the downstairs hall. Elizabeth Harper was wringing her hands disconsolately.

"If only my dear husband were alive," she said miserably.

"Well, he isn't," snapped her irate sister, "and we have to fend for ourselves."

Agatha Winston's hand closed over her umbrella handle with the grip of a warrior on his battle sword.

"There's work to be done," she said, her angry voice threatening in the Kellville house.

Chapter Seven

"**S**top that kicking!"

Jimmy Coles' right foot stopped thumping against the chair leg and hooked quickly around the back of his left ankle as his eyes lifted in a cautious glance at his father. His fork hovered shakily near his mouth, a piece of meat impaled on its tines.

Then his father's cup slammed down furiously and made everyone at the table start.

"*Yes, sir,*" demanded Matthew Coles.

"Yes, sir," Jimmy's faint voice echoed his father's outraged prompting.

"You had better learn your manners, young man," his father said, his voice threatening slow, "or you'll feel the strap across your legs."

Jimmy swallowed the suddenly tasteless beef and sat petrified on his chair, blue eyes staring at his father. Mrs. Coles looked toward her younger son with that look of futile despair which, so often, showed on her face.

Now Matthew Coles picked up his fork and dug it ruthlessly into a thick slice of beef. Shearing off a piece with one tense drawing motion of his knife, he shoved the meat into his mouth and sat chewing it with rhythmic, angry movements of his jaw.

"In my day," he went on as though he had just uttered

his previous comment on the subject, "we valued the honor of our women. We defended it."

Robby sat picking listlessly at his food, his stomach still queasy from the brief fight. He hadn't wanted to sit down with his family at supper but his father had insisted.

"You're not eating, sir," Matthew Coles told him.

Robby looked up at his father. "I don't feel well, sir," he said quietly.

"You shouldn't feel well," his father drove home another lance. "Your intended bride is insulted and you do nothing."

"Matthew, please don't—" Jane Coles started imploringly.

Her husband directed one of his women-were-not-created-to-speak looks at her and she lowered her head, the sentence unfinished. She had been tensely worried ever since Robby had told his father the reason for the fight with John Benton. She knew her husband; knew his unyielding strength and was afraid of what he might badger Robby into doing.

"This is something which must be spoken of," Matthew Coles went on firmly. "And it *will* be spoken of. There will be no shrinking from the truth in my house. I hope I shall never see the day when men no longer defend the honor of their women. How would you like it, ma'm, if I refused to defend your honor against insults?"

Mrs. Coles said nothing. She knew that Matthew wanted no reply but preferred the advantage of asking challenging questions which were not answered. She knew it gave him the pleasure of unopposed refuting.

"No, you have no answer," said Matthew Coles with a tense nodding of his head. "You know as well as I do that when men cease to defend their women and their homes, our society will cease to exist."

Robby drank a little water and felt it trickle coldly into his near-empty stomach. He hoped his father would go on ranting at his mother, beleaguering Jimmy—anything except stay on the subject of Louisa and John Benton. He'd been on it all afternoon at the shop where he'd insisted that Robby perform his usual tasks, ill or not.

"That a son of mine," said Matthew Coles grimly, "should be afraid to stand up for the honor of his intended bride." He shook his head. "Especially since the poor girl has no family man to speak for her." He shook his head again. "In *my* day . . . ," he mused solemnly, probing at his beef with fork stabs.

"May I be excused?" Robby asked.

"You may not, sir," said his father. "The meal is not over."

"Does your stomach still hurt, dear?" Mrs. Coles asked Robby gently.

An attempted smile twitched at the corners of Robby's lips. "I feel better, mother," he said.

"Is there anything I can get for—"

"Don't coddle the boy!" her husband broke in furiously. "Are we raising daughters or sons? It's no wonder he's too cowardly to face John Benton, the way you've coddled and protected him!"

"Matthew, he *did* tell John Benton to leave Louisa alone," she said, the faint spark of resistance born of her defending love for Robby.

"Is that what you call defending honor!" shouted Matthew Coles, his face suddenly livid with fury at being contradicted. "Getting hit in the stomach and whining like a dog all day!"

Jane Coles looked disturbedly toward Jimmy who was staring at his father, his slender body unconsciously cringed away from Matthew Coles' imperious presence.

"Matthew, the—"

"What is this—a house of *women*!" her husband raged on. "Why don't you teach them how to cook and sew!"

"Matthew, the boy," his wife pleaded, a break in her tired voice.

"Don't tell me about the boy! It's time he learned the place of a man in his society!" His head snapped over and he looked accusingly at Jimmy. "Don't think you're going to live your life without fighting," he said to the white-faced boy. "Don't think you're going to get away without defending the honor of your women."

He leaned forward suddenly, neck cords bulging, dark eyes digging into the young boy.

"Tell me, sir," he said with thinly disguised calm, "what would you do if a man insulted your mother?"

"Matthew," his wife begged in anguish, "please . . ."

"Would you just sit by and let the insult pass? Is that what you'd do?" He finished in a sudden burst that made Jimmy's cheek twitch.

"N-no, sir," the boy mumbled.

"Speak up, sir, speak up! You're a man, not a woman, and a man is supposed to be heard!"

"*Yes*, sir."

"Is that what you'd do; let the insult pass?"

"No, no," Jimmy said hurriedly.

"No, what?"

"No, I wouldn't let the—"

"*No, sir.*"

Jimmy bit at his lower lip, a rasping sob shaking in his throat.

"Woman!" cried Matthew Coles. "A house of women!"

"Matthew . . ." His wife's voice was weak and shaking.

Matthew Coles drew in a deep, wavering breath and sawed savagely at his meat. He crammed it into his mouth and started chewing while his family sat tensely in their places, unable to eat.

"*Stop that sniveling*," Matthew Coles said in a low, menacing voice. Jimmy caught his breath and hastily brushed aside the tears that welled in his eyes, dripping down across his freckled cheeks.

"Eat your food," said Matthew Coles. "I don't buy food to be wasted."

Jimmy picked up his fork with shaking fingers and tried to retrieve a piece of potato which kept rolling off the tines. He bit his lip to stop the sobbing and stuck the fork into a piece of meat.

"What would you do?" his father asked.

Jimmy looked over, his face twisted again with frightened apprehension. Robby looked up from his plate, his jaw whitening in repressed anger.

"Well, answer me," Matthew Coles said in a level voice, his fury mollified by the silence of his family. "Would you let some man insult your mother?"

Jane Coles turned her head away abruptly so her sons would not see the mask of sickened anguish it had become.

"N-no, sir," Jimmy said, his stomach turning, tightening.

"What would you do?" Matthew Coles didn't look at his son. He ate his beef and potatoes and drank his coffee, all the time staring into space as if the discussion were of no importance to him. But they could all sense the threat of violence beneath the level of his spoken words.

"I . . . I don't know."

"Don't *know*, sir?" asked his father, voice rising a little.

"I'd, I'd, I'd—"

"Stop-that-stuttering."

"I'd *fight* him," Jimmy blurted out, trying desperately to find the answer that would placate his father.

"Fight him, sir, with your fists?" Matthew Coles stopped chewing a moment and looked pointedly toward his nerve-taut son.

"I, I—"

"With your *fists*?" said his father, loudly.

"I'd get a gun and—"

The hissing catch of breath in his mother's throat made Jimmy stop suddenly and glance toward her with frightened eyes.

Matthew Coles looked intently at Robby, still addressing his younger son.

"You'd get a gun?" he questioned. "Is that what you said, sir?"

"Matthew, what are you trying to—"

"You'd get a gun, you say?" Matthew Coles' rising voice cut off the tortured question of his wife. "A gun?"

"Oh, leave him alone!" Robby burst out with sudden nerve-snapped vehemence. "It's me you're after, talk to me!"

Matthew Coles' nostrils flared out and it appeared, for a moment, that he would explode in Robby's face.

Then a twitching shudder ran down his straight back and he looked down to his food, face graven into a hard, expressionless mold.

"I don't talk to cowards," said Matthew Coles.

Chapter Eight

The Reverend Omar Bond was working on the notes for his Sunday sermon when he heard the front doorbell tinkling. He looked up from his desk, a touch of sorrowing martyrdom in his expression. He *had* hoped no one would call tonight; there was so much necessary work to be done on the sermon.

"Oh my," he muttered to himself as he sat listening to his wife, Clara, come bustling from the kitchen. He heard her nimble footsteps moving down the hall, then the sound of the front door being opened.

"Why, good evening, Miss Winston," he heard Clara say and his face drew into melancholy lines. Of all his parishioners, Miss Winston was the one who most tried his Christian fortitude. There were times when he would definitely have enjoyed telling her to—

"Ah, Miss Winston," he said, smiling beneficently as he rose from his chair. "How good of you to drop by." He ignored the tight sinking in his stomach as being of uncharitable genre. Extending his hand, he approached the grim-faced woman and felt his fingers in her cool, almost manlike grip.

"Reverend," she said, dipping her head but once.

"Do sit down, Miss Winston," the Reverend Bond invited, the smile still frozen on his face.

"May I take your shawl?" Clara Bond asked politely and Agatha Winston shook her head.

"I'll only be a moment," she said.

The Reverend Omar Bond could not check the heartfelt hallelujah in his mind although he masked it well behind his beaming countenance.

He settled down on the chair across from where Miss Winston sat poised on the couch edge as though ready to spring up at a moment's provocation. Clara Bond left the room quietly.

"Is this a social visit?" the Reverend Bond inquired pleasantly, knowing it wasn't.

"No, it is not, Reverend," said Agatha Winston firmly. "It concerns one of your parishioners."

Oh, my God, she's at it again, the Reverend Bond thought with a twinge. Agatha Winston was forever coming to him with stories about his parishioners, nine tenths of which were usually either distorted or completely untrue.

"Oh?" he asked blandly. "Who is that, Miss Winston?"

"*John Benton.*" Agatha Winston rid herself of the given and family names as though they were spiders in her mouth.

"But, I . . ." the Reverend Bond stopped talking, his face mildly shocked. "John Benton?" he said. "Surely not."

"He has asked my niece, Louisa Harper, to . . ." Miss Winston hesitated, searching for the proper phrase, ". . . to *meet* him."

Omar Bond raised graying eyebrows, his hands clasped tightly in his lap.

"How do you know this thing?" he asked, a little less amiably now.

"I know it because my niece told me so," she answered firmly.

The Reverend Bond sat silently a moment, his eyes looking at Miss Winston with emotionless detachment.

"And it's worse than just that," Miss Winston went on, quickly. "It would be one thing if the incident were known only to those immediately concerned. But almost the entire *town* knows of it!"

"I've heard nothing of it," said the Reverend, blandly.

"Well . . ." Agatha Winston was not refuted. "Begging your pardon, Reverend, but . . . well, I don't think anyone would pass along gossip to *you*."

Someone would, thought Omar Bond, looking at Miss Winston with an imperceptible sigh.

"But this makes no earthly sense," he said then. "John Benton is a fine man, a regular churchgoer and, moreover, an extremely respected man in Kellville."

"Be that as it may." Miss Winston's mouth was a lipless gash as she spoke. "My niece's honor has been *insulted* by him."

The Reverend Bond rubbed worried fingers across his smooth chin and, behind his spectacles, his blue eyes were harried.

"It's . . . such a difficult thing to believe," he said quietly, groping for some argument. Agatha Winston always made him feel so defenseless.

"The truth is the truth," stated Miss Winston slowly and clearly. "Believe me, Reverend, when I tell you that if I were a man, I wouldn't be here *talking* about this shocking thing. I'd get myself a horsewhip and—"

She broke off as the Reverend raised a pacifying hand.

"My dear Miss Winston," he said, concernedly, "reason, not violence; is that not what our Lord has taught us?"

The colorless skin rippled slightly over Agatha Winston's taut cheeks. There were definitely times when Christianity did more to thwart than aid, she felt. This was one of the times when she would have preferred a more hardened ethic; this loving humility had its limitations.

But she nodded once, tight-lipped, not wishing to alienate the head of local church activities.

"I came here because I am a woman," she said. "Because I am helpless to do anything by myself."

Christianity does not become you—the Reverend Bond was unable to prevent the thought from shaking loose its repressive bonds. Once again, he hid the thought behind the mild and wrinkled facade he almost always presented to the world.

"Isn't it possible this gossip is exaggerated?" he suggested then. "You know how some people talk. A chance meeting between Benton and your niece might be construed in an entirely false manner."

"I would agree with you," said Agatha Winston, lying, "if it were not for the fact that Louisa, herself, verified the story."

"Oh," he said, cornered again, "Louisa . . . herself."

"Believe me, Reverend, when I say I no more wanted to believe this ugly thing when I first heard of it than you want to believe it now. I'm not the sort of woman who accepts every scrap of gossip as the truth, you know that."

I do not know that, Omar Bond reflected silently, his sad eyes on the face of Agatha Winston.

"Before I accepted one word of this terrible story, I went directly to my niece and questioned her most carefully."

She stiffened her back, fingers tightening in the lap of her black skirt. "*The story is true,*" she declared.

The Reverend Bond licked his upper lip slowly. He started to say something, then exhaled slowly instead while Miss Winston sat waiting for him to call down the wrath of church and Lord upon the head of John Benton.

"What exactly," asked the Reverend Bond, "did Louisa say?"

The thin eyebrows of Agatha Winston pressed down over unpleasantly curious eyes.

"Say?" she asked, not certain of what the Reverend was getting at.

"Yes. Surely, you verified her story?"

"I told you," she said tensely, "I asked her if the incident were true and she said it was."

"Was she upset?"

Agatha Winston looked more unpleasantly confused. "Of course, she was upset," she said. "Her honor was insulted; naturally, she was upset. Especially when I told her how her intended husband, Robby Coles, fought John Benton in defense of her."

The Reverend Bond strained forward, his face suddenly concerned. "Fought?" he asked. "Not . . . not with . . . *guns*?" His voice tapered off in a shocked whisper.

"No, not with guns," Miss Winston said. "Although—"

The look on the Reverend Bond's face kept her from continuing but she knew that he was fully conscious of what she had been about to say.

"What I am getting at," Omar Bond continued, preferring to overlook her probable remark, "is that . . . well, Louisa is very young, very impressionable."

"I don't see how—"

"Let me explain, Miss Winston. Please."

Agatha Winston leaned back, eyes distrusting on the Reverend's face.

"John Benton is what you might call . . . oh, an *idol* in this town, is he not?" asked Bond.

"Men shall not bow down before idols," declared Miss Winston.

The Reverend Bond controlled himself.

"I mean to say, he is extremely admired. I do not, for a moment, say that I condone admiration for a man which is based primarily on an awe of his skill with instruments of death. However . . . this does not alter the fact that, among the younger people particularly, John Benton has achieved almost a . . . a legendary status."

She did not nod or speak or, in any way, indicate agreement.

"I have seen myself," the Reverend Bond went on, "in the church—young boys and girls staring at him with . . . shall we say, unduly fascinated eyes?"

"I do not—"

"Please, Miss Winston, I shall be finished in a moment. To continue: From the vantage point of my pulpit, I have seen your own niece looking so at John Benton."

Miss Winston closed her eyes as if to shut away the thought. "I can hardly believe this," she said, stiffly.

"I say it in no condemning way," the Reverend Bond hastened to explain. "It is a thoroughly natural reaction in the young. I would not even have mentioned it were it not for what you have just told me."

"I don't understand," said Agatha Winston. "Are you telling me that Louisa *lied*? That her story is a deliberate *falsehood*?"

"No, *no*," the Reverend said gently, a smile softening his features, "not a lie. Call it rather a . . . a daydream spoken aloud."

Miss Winston rose irately.

"Reverend, I'm shocked that you should stand up for John Benton, a man who lives by violence. And I'm hurt—*deeply* hurt that you should accuse my niece of deliberately *lying*."

The Reverend Bond rose quickly and moved toward her.

"My dear Miss Winston," he said, "I *assure* you . . ."

Agatha Winston brushed away a tear which had, somehow, managed to force its way out of her eye duct. A sob rasped dryly in her lean throat.

"I came to you because there is nothing my sister and her daughter can do to defend their good name. But instead of—"

Another sob, dry and harsh.

Against his better judgment, the Reverend Omar Bond found himself standing before Agatha Winston, explaining, apologizing.

"I'll tell you what I'll do," he finally said, growing desperate with her. "I'll ride out personally to John Benton's ranch and speak to him."

"He'll deny it," Agatha Winston said, agitatedly. "Do you think he'll—"

"Miss Winston, if the incident occurred as you said, John Benton will admit it," the Reverend Bond said firmly. "That's all I can say for now. I sympathize with your situation, I most certainly will speak out Sunday against the insidious cruelty of this gossiping." He gestured weakly. "And . . . and I'll go out to see John Benton in the morning."

He was leading her to the door finally.

"Please don't upset yourself, Miss Winston," he told her, "I am confident we can work it out to the satisfaction of all."

"Oh, if only there were a *man* in our family to speak for us," Agatha Winston said, vengefully.

"I will speak for you," said Bond. "Remember, my child, we are all one family under God."

Frankly, Miss Winston did not accept that tenet of Christianity. Her mind pushed the concept aside angrily as she strode off into the night, unsatisfied.

The Reverend Omar Bond shut the door and turned back as Clara came out of the kitchen, drying her hands.

"What's wrong, dear?" she asked, concernedly.

"Offhand, I should say the qualifications for membership in the church," said the Reverend Bond with a weary shake of his head.

Chapter Nine

The hooves of the black roan thudded slowly down the long darkness of Armitas Street, headed for the square. Robby Coles sat slumped in the saddle, his rein-holding hands clasped loosely over the horn. He was staring ahead bleakly, between the bobbing ears of his mount, watching the dark street jog toward him, then disappear beneath the legs of the roan. His lips were pressed together; his entire face reflected the tense nervousness he felt.

When supper had ended, he'd grabbed his hat and gunbelt and started for the door, not wanting to listen to his father anymore.

"Where are you going?" Matthew Coles had asked.

"For a ride," he'd answered.

"You'd better not," his father said, "you might run into John Benton and then you'd have to come running home and hide in the closet."

Robby didn't say anything. He just jerked open the door and went out, seeing from the corners of his eyes his mother looking at him, one frail hand at her breast.

Then, halfway to the stable, Robby heard the back door open and shut quickly.

"*Son*," his father called.

Robby didn't want to stay. He felt like jumping on his horse and galloping out the alleyway before his father could say another word. But open defiance was not in him; he might flare up now and then under provocation but, inevitably, he obeyed his father. He was twenty-one and, supposedly, his own man; but those twenty-one years of rigid training still kept him bound.

He stood there silently, buckling on his gun belt as his father's boots came crunching over the hard ground of the yard. He felt Matthew Coles' hand close over his shoulder.

"Son, I didn't mean to rile you," Matthew Coles said, his voice no longer hard. "It's been a hard day and I'm out of sorts. You can understand that, son."

Robby could feel himself drawing back. Whenever his father called him *son* . . .

"Yes, sir," he said. "I . . . understand."

"I didn't intend to blow up at the table like that," Matthew Coles went on. "I believe a family meal should be eaten in peace."

"Yes, sir," Robby said, thinking of the countless meals that had degenerated into stomach-wrenching agonies because of his father's temper.

"It's just that . . . well." His father gestured with his free hand. "Just that you're my son and I want to be proud of you."

"Yes, sir." The tight, crawling sensation still mounted in Robby's stomach. Don't, he thought, *don't*; his eyes staring at the dark outline of his father's head.

"I don't want to force you into anything, son," said Matthew Coles in as understanding a voice as he could manage. "You're of age and I can't make you do anything your mind is set against."

Robby started to speak, then closed his mouth without a word. His father wasn't through yet.

"I can punish your younger brother if he does something I know is wrong." Matthew Coles shook his head once, slowly. "I can't do that with you, son," he said. "You're of age and your life is your own; your decisions are your own."

Suddenly, Robby wished his father would rage again, rant and yell. It was easier to fight that.

"But I don't believe you realize, son," said Matthew Coles, his voice a steady, coercive flow. "This is a very serious matter. I couldn't talk about it at the table because of your mother and your younger brother. It's not the sort of subject men discuss over a family supper table."

Now his father's arm was around his shoulders and, as they ambled slowly toward the stable, Robby could feel his stomach muscles trembling and he had to clench his hands to keep the fingers steady.

"Son," his father said, "there are certain things a man must face in this life. I don't say these things are just or fair . . . or even reasonable. But they're a part of our life and no man can avoid them." Matthew Coles paused for emphasis. "And the most important of those," he said, "is that a man defend his home and defend his family."

But she's not my family. Robby wanted to say it but he was afraid to.

"I . . . want to do what's right," he said instead, his throat feeling dry and tight, the gun at his waist seeming very heavy. He wished he hadn't taken the gun with him. What if he ran into John Benton and Benton had a gun on too?

"Of course, you want to do what's right, son," said Matthew Coles, nodding. "You're a Coles and the men of our family have always done what's right—what *has* to be done."

They were in the darkness of the stable now. Robby could smell the odor of damp hay and hear the soft stamping of the two horses in their stalls. He heard his roan nicker quietly and it made him swallow nervously. I'll ride you when I'm ready, he thought belligerently as if the horse had asked to be ridden toward town, toward the possibility of meeting Benton.

"Sit down, son," Robby heard the firm voice of his father say. Weakly, he sank down on the wooden bench and his father sat down beside him, arm still around Robby's lean shoulders.

His father's voice kept on, seeming to surround Robby in the cool, damp-smelling blackness of the stable.

"I know that, strictly speaking, Louisa Harper is not yet a part of our family. And, if there were men folks alive in her family now, I would say no more. It would be *their* responsibility to defend her honor."

Honor. Honor—the word thumped dully in Robby's mind as he stared straight ahead, listening.

"However," said Matthew Coles, "there *are* no men left in the Harper family. There are no men left in the Winston family which was the family that Louisa's mother was born to."

I know all that, Robby thought, trying hard not to shiver. He said quietly, "Yes, sir."

"And because there are no men in Louisa Harper's family, the responsibility must shift itself to you. Since the young lady is your intended bride, you are the only one who can defend her name."

Silence then. Robby felt his father's hand pat once-twice on his shoulder as if to say—You see then, it's settled, now go out and shoot John Benton.

"But . . . well, I . . . what about what I said to Benton?" Robby asked.

"Your conversation with Benton, you mean?" his father said, without expression.

Robby's throat moved quickly. "Well . . . it was more than just a conversation, sir. I told him in . . . in no uncertain terms that if he didn't leave Louisa alone, I'd—"

"*Son,*" Matthew Coles interrupted in a slow, firm voice, "the damage has been done. This is not a situation which can be settled by talk. John Benton attempted to arrange an immoral meeting with your intended bride. Son, the facts are clear."

"But, Louisa didn't say—"

"Sir?"

Robby felt his throat muscles tighten at the slight but very certain stiffening in his father's voice. But he knew he had to go on or he'd be cornered and defenseless.

"Sir, Louisa didn't say that Benson tried to arrange an . . ." he swallowed, "an *immoral* meeting."

"Son," his father said, almost sadly it seemed, "you are a grown man, not a child. For what purpose do you suppose John Benton requested a meeting?"

Robby drew in a ragged breath; answerless.

"There is only one question involved here," Matthew Coles completed his case, "and that is—do you mean to defend the honor of your intended bride or do you mean to let yourself be judged a coward—for, believe me, sir, you *will* be judged a coward and the meanest sort of coward—a man who will not stand up for his woman."

Robby's head sank forward, his heart beating heavily, his hands pressed tightly together in his lap.

"I want to do what's . . . what's right, sir," he said huskily. "But—"

"Of course you do," his father said, arm tightening around Robby's shoulder. "Of course you do, sir."

Abruptly, his father was up on his feet, looking down at Robby.

"I will leave the working out of this to you," he said. "You are a man and a man must do things his own way."

Robby tried to say something but he couldn't.

"I would suggest, however," said his father, "that, for tonight anyway, you leave your gun at home. For if you should run into John Benton and he be armed . . ."

Robby shivered in the darkness, his body slumped on the hard wooden bench. His stomach hurt again.

"You're not in good physical form tonight," his father continued. "I think you should wait until—"

"Sir, I'll do what I think is right but . . ." Robby swallowed convulsively. "Let me . . . m-make my own plans." His voice was thin and shaking in the darkness.

His father pretended not to hear the nervous fear in his son's voice.

"The problem is yours, sir," he said in a satisfied voice. He patted Robby briskly on the shoulder. "I will say no more—to anyone." Pause. "You know exactly what has to be done."

Then his father had turned and Robby was watching the dark shadow of him moving for the yard.

At the door, his father looked back.

"Don't be too late," he said. "Remember, there's a good deal of work to be done at the shop tomorrow."

Matthew Coles turned away and Robby listened to the crunching of his boots on the ground, then the measured clumping up the porch steps, the opening and closing of the back door.

In the silence, a shaking breath caught in Robby's throat. He sat there for a long time, staring into the blackness with hopeless eyes.

Then, after a while, he stood, unbuckled his gun belt and left it hanging on a nail.

Now he was riding slowly down Armitas Street, staring ahead, his hands clenched around the horn. He didn't want to go into town; he was afraid of seeing anyone. But, even less, did he want to go into the house and see his father. Because, in spite of what had been said, Robby wasn't sure whether he was going to put on a gun against Benton. It was simply that he didn't want to die. It was simply that honor seemed a very little thing beside life.

Robby tilted back his head and looked up into the jet expanses of the sky, sprinkled with glowing star dots. He felt the rhythmic jogging of the horse beneath him as he watched the sky.

Those are the stars, he thought. They were so far away no man could ever count the miles, much less travel them. It gave him a strange feeling to watch them and know how far away they were and how big. Once, his school teacher had told Robby that if a man could gallop a horse as fast as possible and keep on galloping all his life, he still wouldn't even travel a thousandth of the way to a star. So far away they were and he was so small and what he did was so unimportant to the stars. Why was it so important to him then?

Robby Coles looked down quickly at the darkness of the earth. It was no use looking at stars. Stars couldn't save him; he had to save himself.

He saw that his roan was walking past the first stores of downtown Kellville and his hands lifted from the horn to guide the horse right at the next intersection. He didn't want to ride into the square. Someone might see him; someone who knew.

When Robby turned onto St. Virgil Street, the horseman came out of the night toward him.

For a moment, Robby felt a cold, rippling sensation in his groin that made him twitch. It's *him*, the thought lashed at his mind. He almost jerked the horse around and fled. Then, with a sudden stiffening, he lowered his head and looked intently at the saddle horn, feeling the roan bump steadily beneath him, hearing the thud of the approaching hoofbeats. He can't shoot if I'm not looking at him, his mind thought desperately, no one shoots a man that isn't looking. His heart beat faster and harder, sweat broke out thinly on his forehead. The horse came closer. You don't shoot a man when he's not looking!— he thought in anguish—you never shoot a man when he's—

The horseman rode by without a word and Robby sagged forward weakly in the saddle, lips trembling, breath caught in his throat.

It was no use, no use; he realized it then. He couldn't fight Benton; the very thought petrified him. No matter what happened, no matter what anyone said, he couldn't fight Benton. He *wouldn't* fight him.

A heavy breath faltered between Robby's parted lips. In a way, it was relieving to make the decision. It gave him a settled feeling. Even realizing that he'd have to face his father with the decision, it made him feel better.

As he rode for the edge of town, Robby wondered what Louisa would want him to do. She certainly seemed astounded that morning when he paled and went storming from the house after she told him about Benton asking her for a meeting. No, he didn't think Louisa would expect him to fight Benton with a gun.

Yet, what if she did? He loved her and felt responsible for her. His father had been right in that respect anyway. Someone had to defend her and he seemed to be the only one to do it.

But did he have to *die* for her honor?

Robby nudged his boot heels into the roan's flanks and the big horse broke into a rocking-chair canter up St. Virgil Street toward the edge of Kellville.

The horsemen seemed to appear from nowhere. One moment, Robby was alone, riding in his thoughts. The next, three horses were milling around him and he was cringing with frightened surprise in his saddle.

"Hey, Robby," one of the young men shouted above the stirring hooves of the four horses.

Robby swallowed. "Oh . . . hello," he said, recognizing the voice of Dave O'Hara, an old school friend of his he hadn't seen more than three times in the past year.

The horses twisted around, snorting, while Robby stared at O'Hara's dark form.

"Where ya goin'?" O'Hara asked.

"No place."

"What's that?"

"*No* place!"

"Well, come on with us then. We're headin' for the Zorilla."

Robby hesitated long enough for O'Hara to lean forward and look intently at him.

"You goin' after Benton, Robby?" O'Hara asked, almost eagerly.

It felt like someone driving a cold fist against his heart. Robby jolted in the saddle with a grunt they didn't hear because of the milling horses.

"N-no," he faltered, "I—"

"Heard what he done to your girl," O'Hara said grimly. "You ain't lettin' him get *away* with that, are you?"

It was like a nightmare—sitting in darkness on the shifting saddle, watching the three horsemen move about him in the jerky little movements caused by their restless mounts, hearing the deep-chested snortings of their horses.

"No, I'm ... going to do what ..." Robby's mind searched desperately for an answer that wouldn't commit him. Then he grew nervous at his own revealing hesitation and finished quickly.

"I'll do what has to be done," he said, his voice sounding thin and strengthless.

"Damn right," O'Hara said vengefully and the other two men said something between themselves. "The bastard's got a slug comin' for what he done. Him and his damn *rep*. Why'd he leave the Rangers anyhow? And, he's so brave, why don't he tote no gun?" O'Hara's voice was tight with a bitter jealousy. He was one of Kellville's young men who had made the inevitable step from idolizing Benton to envying and hating him.

Robby sat his mount numbly, hearing the voice of Dave O'Hara as if it were a million miles away.

"When you goin' for him, Robby?"

Robby bit his teeth together. "I ..."

The three riders watching him, Dave O'Hara and the other two. When are you going for him? When are you going to die? A shudder ran down Robby's back. Then he stiffened himself.

"When the time comes," he said, his voice unnaturally loud.

The dark riders still moved around him. "Well, that's your own business, Robby," O'Hara said, "but I want ya to know we're all behind ya. Everybody knows Benton's a dirty coward who's too *yella* to tote a gun. And after what he done to your girl . . . well, there ain't nothin' more to say."

"That's right," Robby said, feeling as if he were trapped there with the three of them. "There's nothing more."

"Well how about headin' for the Zorilla with us and let me buy ya a drink?"

"No, I . . . have to get home." Loudly, forcedly. "I was just on an errand for my father."

"Oh . . ." O'Hara punched him lightly on the arm. "We're all behind ya, Robby," he said, almost happily. "Ain't a man in town that ain't behind ya. When the time comes . . ." Another punch. "We'll back ya."

They were gone in a clouding of night dust. Robby waited a moment, then twisted around in his saddle and saw the three of them spurring for the square.

How did the story get around so *fast*? Robby couldn't understand it. Only three men had seen the fight outside of Pat and Pat wasn't the kind to spread tales.

It was horrible how fast the story was traveling. And now he'd be trapped further, now O'Hara and his two friends would tell everybody that he was going to get John Benton.

"*No.*" Robby couldn't keep the shaking word from escaping his lips. No, he didn't want to fight Benton, he didn't *want* to! A shudder ran down his back and he couldn't seem to get enough air in his lungs to breathe.

Ten minutes to nine, Kellville, Texas, September 12, 1879. The end of the first day.

The Second Day

Chapter Ten

Benton was riding fence. There were only three men working for him and he couldn't afford to spare any of them for this simple but hour-consuming chore. Mounted on his blood bay, Socks, so named for the whiteness of its feet extending to the fetlocks, Benton was riding leisurely along the rutted trail that preceding fence rides had worn.

Five times during the morning, he'd stopped to fix loose or broken wires, missing staples, once a sagging post. Each time, he'd gotten the supplies he needed from the saddle-fastened pouch in which were staples, a hatchet, a pair of wire cutters, and a coil of stay wire.

Finding a fence section that needed repairs, Benton would ease himself off the bay and ground the open reins. Socks would then remain in place without being tied while his master worked. The work completed, Benton would take hold of the reins and raise the stiffness of his batwing chaps over the saddle.

"Come on, churnhead," he would say softly and the bay would start along the line again.

Benton's horse was one of the two cutting horses in the ranch's small remuda, a bridle-wise gelding that Benton had spent over a year in training. Cutting was a ticklish and difficult job, the most exacting duty any horse could be called upon to perform. It demanded of the mount an apex of physical and mental control plus a calm dispatch that would not panic the animal being cut from the herd. A cutting horse had to spin and turn as quickly as the cow, always edging the reluctant animal away from the herd without frightening it. This twisting and turning entailed much good riding too and, although Benton had ridden since he was eight, the process of sitting a cutting horse had taken all the ability he had.

Benton knew he rode Socks on jobs that any ordinary cowhorse could manage. But he was extremely fond of the bay and never demanded a great deal of it outside of its cutting duties. Riding fence was no effort for the bay. It enjoyed the ambling walk with its master in the warm, sunlight-brimming air. Benton would pat the bay's neck as they rode.

"Hammerhead," he'd tell the horse, "someday we'll all be rich and ride to town in low-necked clothes and have thirty hands workin' for us."

The bay would snort its reply and Benton would pat it again and say, "You're all right, fuzz tail."

When Benton rode the range, he wore a converted Colt-Walker .44 at his left side, butt forward. Sometimes it seemed as if it even worried Julia for him to wear a gun around the ranch.

"Honey, you want a snake to kill me?" he'd say with a grin.

"I don't want *any*thing to kill you," she'd answer grimly. "Or any*body*."

That day, while riding fence, Benton reached across his waist and drew out the pistol with an easy movement. He held it loosely in his hand and looked at its smooth metal finish, the notches of the cylinder, the curved trigger in its heavy guard.

He often found himself looking at the Colt; it was the only thing he had that really reminded him of the old days. He'd killed nine men with this pistol in the line of Ranger duty. There was Jack Kramer in Trinity

City, Max Foster outside of Comanche, Rebel Dean, Johnny Ostrock, Bob Melton, Sam and Barney Dobie, Aaran Graham's two sons; nine men lying in their graves because of the mechanism in this four-pound piece of apparatus.

Benton hefted the pistol in his palm, wondering if he missed the old days, wondering if violence had become a part of him. He slipped his finger into the guard and spun the pistol around backward and forward in the old way, then shoved it back into its holster with a quick, blurred movement of his hand. Miss it, *hell.* He was alive, he had a good little layout, a wonderful wife; one day there would be children—that was enough for any man.

He was grateful the percentages had passed over him. By Ranger standards he had outlived himself at least five times. Another month in the service, another year maybe and he would have died like the others, like the many others. As horrible as it had been, the incident with Graham and his sons had spared him that.

Benton threw back his shoulders and took a deep breath of the clean air. Life, he thought, that's what counts; killing is for animals.

He found the trapped calf near the spring. It was stuck under the fence where it had tried to wriggle through a gap caused by water erosion. Benton could hear the loud quaver of its bawling a half mile away. He nudged his flower rowels across the bay's flanks and the horse broke into an easy trot down the trail.

The calf looked up at Benton's approach, its big, dark eyes wild with fright. Its back hooves kicked futilely at the earth, spraying dirt over the long grass.

Benton jumped down from the bay, grounded the reins, and started for the calf, a grin on his face.

"Hello, you old acorn," he said. "Runnin' off to the city again?"

The calf bawled loudly and kicked again at the scoured ground.

"All right, little girl," Benton said, drawing on the gloves he'd pulled from his back Levi's pocket, "take it easy now. Poppa will get you out."

He hunkered down beside the fence and the calf complained loudly as Benton grabbed the wire that held it pinned down, the sharp barbs embedded deeply in its skin and flesh.

"Easy now, deacon," Benton spoke soothingly as he tried to draw out the barbs so he could raise the taut wire. He grimaced slightly as the calf squalled loudly, blood oozing across its spotted back. "*Ea*-sy now, little girl, we'll get you out in no time."

Fifteen minutes later, the bay was moving across the range, leading the roped yearling. Benton glanced back and grinned at the tugging calf.

"Gotta get your wounds fixed, runty," he told the yearling, then turned back with a shake of his head. The calf's mother had died the previous winter and the calf had been more trouble than it was worth since then, having to be fed because water and grass were still too heavy a fare for its young stomach and, invariably, wandering from the herd and getting lost.

"We're goin' to sell you for boot leather, acorn," Benton said lightly, not even looking back. "That's what we're goin' to sell you for."

The calf dragged along behind, sulky and complaining.

Back at the ranch, Benton led the calf into the barn and salved up its back, then turned it loose in the corral.

The rig was standing in front of the house as he walked toward it. It looked familiar but he wasn't sure where he'd seen it before. He moved in long strides across the yard and went into the kitchen. He was getting a drink of cool water from the dipper when Julia came in.

"Who's visitin'?" he asked.

"The Reverend Bond," she said.

"Oh? What's *he* want?"

"He came to see you."

Benton looked at Julia curiously. "What for?" he asked.

Julia shook her head once. "He won't tell me," she said. "But I think I know."

"What?"

Julia turned to the stove. "Well, from the way he avoided the subject, I'd say that story."

"What story?"

"About Louisa Harper and you."

A look of disgust crossed Benton's face. "Oh, no," he said in a pained voice. "*More?*"

He shook his head and groaned softly to himself as he took off the bull-hide chaps and tossed them on a chair by the door. "Oh . . . blast," he said. "What's goin' on in town anyway?"

At the door, he turned to her. "Aren't you comin' in?" he asked.

"You think I should?" she asked. "The Reverend doesn't seem to think it's anything for me to hear."

He came back to her, his brow lined with curious surprise. "What is it?" he asked. "Don't tell me you're startin' to *believe* this thing?"

Julia swallowed nervously. "Of course not," she said. "It's just that . . ."

He hooked his arm in hers. "Come on, ma," he said amusedly. "In we go."

In the hallway, he pinched her and she whispered, "Stop that!" But the tenseness was gone from her face.

As they entered the small sitting room, the Reverend Omar Bond stood up and extended his hand to Benton with a smile.

"Mr. Benton," he said.

"Reverend." Benton nodded. "Excuse the hand. I been out ridin'."

Bond smiled. "Not at all," he said.

"Sit down, Reverend," Benton said, putting Julia on a chair. "What's on your mind?"

"Well, sir," the Reverend Bond said, "I think that . . ." He hesitated and glanced at Julia.

"That's all right, Reverend," Benton said, smiling guardedly. "My wife knows all about it. Who's been tellin' *you* stories now? Louisa Harper?"

The Reverend Bond looked at Benton, mouth slightly agape. Then a sudden look of relief came over his face and he beamed at both of them.

"I'm so glad," he said quickly. "I didn't believe the story at all and yet . . ." He clucked and shook his head sadly. "Once the poison is put in one's mind, one is hard put to find the adequate antidote of reason."

Benton glanced at his wife. "I know," he said, trying not to smile. "That old suspicious poison."

He sat down on the arm of the chair. "All right now," he said seriously, "who told you this story, Reverend? Robby Coles?"

"No, as a matter of fact it was Louisa's aunt, Miss Agatha Winston," Bond said. "And . . ." he gestured with his hand, "I might add, were this not a situation of such potential gravity, I would not, for a moment, betray a confidence. You understand."

"It'll go no further than this room," Benton said. His mouth hardened. "I wish I could say the same for this damned story."

"John," his wife said quietly. He glanced down at her, then up at the Reverend with a rueful smile. "Pardon," he said, then became absorbed in thought. "Agatha Winston," he mused. "Do I know her?"

"She owns the ladies' clothes shop in town, doesn't she?" Julia asked.

"That's correct." The Reverend Bond nodded. "She came to my house last night and told me that . . . well . . ." He cleared his throat embarrassedly.

"It's quite all right, Reverend," Julia told him.

"Thank you," Bond replied. "To be terribly blunt then, Miss Winston said that your husband tried to arrange for an immoral meeting with her niece. Again," he added quickly, "I would not say such a thing in your presence were I not convinced that the story is untrue."

When Bond had repeated what Agatha Winston had told him, Benton's right hand closed angrily in his lap and his face grew suddenly taut. He sat there stone-faced until Bond had finished talking, then he said in a flat, toneless voice, "And did she say who told her this story?"

Bond nodded his head. "Yes," he answered, "she said that her niece, Louisa, told her. Or, rather, that she had heard the gossip in town and then checked with Louisa to verify the story."

"And Louisa said it was true," Benton said disgust-edly.

Bond gestured with his hands and looked helpless. "That is what she said," he admitted.

Benton exhaled heavily. "Well, it's not true," he said. His eyes raised to Bond's. "Do I have to tell you it's not true?"

"I would like you to," Bond replied, meeting Benton's gaze steadily.

Benton's mouth tightened. "It is not true," he said slowly and Julia put her hand on his with an abrupt movement.

Bond's lips raised in a conciliatory smile. "I'm sorry," he said. "It wasn't that I believed you were guilty. It was just that . . . well, I felt that the situation called for such a definite statement." He leaned forward. "Very well," he said, "we'll say no more of that. What's important now is ending this gossip before it does any more harm. I . . . understand there was some physical conflict yesterday."

Benton nodded then, briefly, told the Reverend about how Robby Coles had come into the Zorilla and started a fight.

"And this was the first you heard of the matter," Bond said.

"That's right," said Benton. "The first."

"I see." Bond nodded as he spoke. "I . . . imagine, then, that it all began with Louisa telling Robby that . . . telling him what she *did* tell him," he finished hastily.

"But why?" Benton asked, irritably baffled. "Does it make any sense?"

Julia smiled a little at the Reverend Bond and he repressed an answering smile. "He really doesn't know," Julia said.

Omar Bond nodded slowly. "I believe it," he said. "Yes, I believe that firmly. Your husband is not the sort of man who indulges himself in false modesty."

"Know what?" Benton asked. "What are you two talking about?"

"What I said to you yesterday, John," Julia said. "Louisa Harper is in love with you."

Benton looked pained again. "Oh . . . come on, Julia," he said.

"I think the assumption is justified," said the Reverend. "You see, Mister Benton, you represent something to the young people of this town. In . . . all honesty," he went on reluctantly, "I must admit that I'm not sure what you represent to them is a . . . healthy thing. Needless to say, I do not, for a moment, think that you still are what they conceive you to be. No, I—"

"What's that, Reverend?" Benton interrupted. "What do they think I am?"

Bond looked embarrassed. "A . . . fearless . . . and a very dangerous man," he faltered. "Mind you, I'm only assuming now. But I think that . . . well, they regard your skill with a gun as one of paramount achievement."

"But I don't *wear* a gun in town," Benton said stiffly. "They've never even seen me with a gun on."

"They've never seen John Hardin either," Bond countered, "but they know what he's done."

The Reverend's face grew sadly reflective. "It was people like this who . . . lined the roads for miles when John Hardin was taken to prison. People who waited for just one momentary glimpse of a man who had killed others with guns." Bond shook his head grimly. "It makes no sense—to me, at any rate—but it *is* so, let us admit it freely; now. Your reputation as a Texas Ranger is immense, Mister Benton. It caused a, perhaps, foolish young girl to become enamored of what she conceived you to be. It caused her, in a moment of . . ." he gestured searchingly with his hands, ". . . shall we say, a moment of *un*thinking delusion, to pretend out loud; unhappily, to pretend in the presence of her intended husband. Perhaps she meant nothing by it; I'm sure she didn't. It was a girlish whim, I imagine, perhaps done to make her intended husband jealous of someone—anyone. Young girls are . . . often misled by their feelings."

Bond leaned back, hands clasped in his lap.

"And I believe it was your reputation—exaggerated as it may be—that caused this event. Believe me, sir, I'm not accusing you of anything but . . . perhaps this is, in some measure, an unfortunate result of the life you formerly led."

"Reverend, is that . . . well, *fair*?" Julia asked. "My husband worked for law, for order. If he killed, it was not for the sake of killing; it was because it was his job."

"My dear lady," said Bond warmly, "I would not, for a moment, accuse your husband of being anything that he is not. That he, voluntarily, chose to put aside violence and live as a peaceful citizen, speaks wonderfully for his character. It is just that . . . well, I must repeat, I fear, were it not for the past events of Mister Benton's life, this situation would not have occurred."

"Well, this is getting us nowhere," Benton said, gruffly. "All right, maybe this Harper girl made up the story. But you said her aunt checked with her. Why didn't the Harper girl tell the truth *then*?"

Bond smiled gently. "You are not acquainted with her aunt, Mister Benton. Miss Winston, though, I cannot deny, a loyal Christian, often shows in her dealings with others more hasty righteousness than understanding. And her niece is very sensitive, very retiring. Cornered . . . frightened, perhaps, she would hardly have confessed that she . . . pretended, shall we say. You can understand that."

"I can understand it," Julia said. "John, you mustn't be angry with her. I'm sure she's more frightened than anything else with the gossip she's started."

"Well, that doesn't do me any good," Benton said. "If *she* doesn't stop the gossip, who can?"

"Perhaps you can," Bond answered.

Benton looked surprised. "How?" he asked.

"I would think that if you rode in to Kellville and spoke to Louisa Harper, spoke to her mother, perhaps to her aunt—the situation might be settled."

Benton looked trapped. "But . . . what good would that do?" he asked. "They seem to have their minds made up already."

"I can think of nothing more direct," Bond said. "If you wish, I could come along as . . . oh, say a middle party to ease tension."

"Reverend, I have a lot of work to do around here," Benton said, his voice rising a little. "I can't go ridin' off to town just like that. This is a small layout; I only have three hands beside myself and that's spreadin' out the labor pretty thin."

"I appreciate that," Bond said, nodding. "But . . . well, this situation could become quite bad. Believe me, I've seen such things happen before. I mean quite bad."

Julia looked up at her husband, her face drawn worriedly. "John," she said, "I think you should."

Benton twisted his shoulders irritably. "But, honey—" He broke off then and exhaled quickly. "All right," he said, "I'll ride in tomorrow and . . . see what I can do."

Bond looked embarrassed. "Well," he said, "I would think that—"

"Reverend, this place is creepin' with work that needs to be done! I just can't *do* it today!"

"John."

Benton looked aside at his wife, his face angrily taut. Then another thin breath fell from his nostrils.

"All right," he said disgustedly, "I'll go in this afternoon. But . . ." He didn't finish but only shook his head sadly.

"I don't think it will take long," Bond told him. "Would, uh, you like me to come with you and . . ."

"No, I'll handle it," Benton said. He managed a brief smile at the Reverend. "I'm thankin' you, Reverend," he said, "but . . . I think I can handle it myself."

Bond smiled. "Fine," he said. "Fine. I think it will all work out splendidly." He stood up. "Well, I . . . really must be getting back to town now."

"Oh, can't you stay for dinner?" Julia asked. "It's almost time."

"I'm afraid not," Bond said, gratefully. "I do thank you, Mrs. Benton, but . . . well." He sighed. "My . . . ranch, too, is overrun with work that needs to be done."

Later, over dinner, Benton shook his head and groaned to himself, thinking about all the work time he was going to lose.

"This is hogwash," he muttered.

"Are you sure you don't want me to come with you?" Julia asked.

Benton shook his head. "No, I'm ridin' in fast. Maybe I can get it settled quick and come back in time to get some work done."

Julia poured in more coffee, then stood beside the

table, smiling down at her husband. After a moment, he looked up at her. A slow grin relaxed his mouth.

"I know," he said, amusedly, "get a haircut."

Julia laughed. "How did you guess?"

Chapter Eleven

He was surrounded by guns. On the wall racks behind him and at his right were rifles—a Springfield .45 caliber breech-loader, a Sharps and Hanker .52 caliber rim-fire carbine, a Henry Deringer rifle, a Colt .44 revolving rifle, a new Sharps-Borschardt .45, three 45/10 nine-shot Winchesters—all of them resting on wooden pegs, their metal glinting in the sunlit brightness of the shop, their stocks glossy with rubbed-in oils.

Across from him, behind his father's bench, was the board on which his father and he hung repaired pistols like a watchmaker hung repaired watches. Dangling by their trigger guards were five Colt revolvers, a Remington .36 caliber Navy pistol, an Allen and Thurber .32 caliber pepperbox, and three .41 caliber Deringer pistols. All of them had tags tied to them which had the names of the owner and the cost of the repair job.

On the bench in front of Robby Coles were the parts of a .44 caliber 1860 Model Colt which he had converted from percussion to cartridge fire by cutting off the rear end of the cylinder and replacing it with a breechblock containing a loading gate and rebounding fire pin. He'd only managed to get a section of it assembled all morning.

He couldn't seem to concentrate, that was the trouble.

Every few moments he'd start thinking about his father or O'Hara or Louisa and his fingers would put down the part he was working on and, for a long time, he'd sit staring across the small shop, brooding.

Then, in the middle of a thought, Robby's eyes would focus suddenly and he'd find himself staring at the pistols hanging across the shop from him. He would sit there, looking at the long-barreled Colts, at their plow-handle shaped stocks, their hammers like steer horns jutting out behind the cylinder, the scimiter triggers filed to a hair.

He'd think of John Benton aiming one of them at him, squeezing the trigger. And, suddenly, he'd shudder in the warm shop and his cheek would be pale. No, he'd think, *no*. And go back to work; or, at least, try to go back to work.

But then, a few minutes later, abruptly, he'd remember the look some men gave him as he rode to work that morning. And his throat would move and the chain of thoughts would begin all over again. He'd end up staring at the pistols on the board again and shuddering. Through ten o'clock, through eleven, through—

Robby's hands twitched on the bench top, dropping the smooth cylinder as heavy footsteps sounded in the doorway. Looking up quickly, Robby saw his father coming across the floor, seeming very tall in his dark suit and hat, his face grave and still. Robby felt his hand start to shake and, around the edge of his stomach, all the muscles and tendons started tightening in like drawn wires.

Matthew Coles stopped by the bench and looked down at the litter of Colt parts across the bench top. He glanced up at Robby, his face a mask of unpleasant surprise.

"Sir?" he said

Robby swallowed. "I'm sorry, father. I . . ."

"I understand your concern with other thoughts, sir,"

said Matthew Coles. "However . . . we have duties to perform in life beside those necessary ones of honor."

"Yes, sir." Robby picked up the cylinder again and started working, hoping that his father would leave it at that.

"I've just come from the bank," said Matthew Coles, removing his dark coat and hanging it up carefully on the clothes tree in a back corner of the shop. "There was talk about the Benton incident. *Hard* talk, sir."

Robby's throat moved again and his teeth gritted together as he kept on trying to work.

"I was asked by several men when you were going to settle this matter." Matthew Coles was adjusting arm garters to keep the sleeves up and away from filings and oil. "I told them," he said, "that it was your decision to make but that I assumed it would be soon."

Robby felt his stomach muscles start throbbing. Then, a bolt of terror numbed him as he felt a betraying looseness around his eyes. He forced his lips together and stared down at the bench without seeing anything, his eyes strained and unblinking.

". . . a matter of honor that needs settling," he heard the tail-end of his father's words but didn't dare reply for fear there would be a break in his voice. His hands fumbled and pretended to work on the cool metal of the Colt parts.

Silence a moment as his father adjusted the apron over his shirt and trouser front, sat down at the other bench, and looked over the disassembled Winchester.

Matthew Coles reached for the long barrel, then glanced up.

"Son, between you and me," he said, "when do you intend to settle this thing? Mind you, I'm not pushing; you're of age and I believe the final decision is yours to make. But the situation is getting more grave by the hour. I heard talk of it all over town. People are expecting this thing of you, sir. And soon."

Robby drew in a ragged breath. "Father, I . . ."

"It's Thursday today," Matthew Coles estimated. "I believe the matter should be settled before the weekend."

Robby's eyes closed suddenly as he bent over his work. A low gasp caught in his throat. No . . . *no*! He bit his shaking lower lip. He was in a corner, everyone was surrounding him, pushing him, demanding.

"I have heard that Louisa Harper is being kept in her house until this situation is cleared up. For myself, I believe that there is no other way. Certainly, she cannot face anyone in the street while the matter goes unsettled."

Stop looking at me! Robby's mind erupted, still working, head down, fingers unable to do more than fumble and slip.

"I spoke to young Jim Bonney," said Matthew Coles. "He agreed with me that your decision to face Benton was the only one possible under the circumstances. However, he also said that, if he were in your place, he would have ended the situation immediately."

Robby swallowed with effort. "Easy for him to talk," he said, without looking up. "He doesn't have to do it."

He didn't even have to look up to know the expression on his father's face. It was the one that said as clearly as if words were spoken—What has that to do with what we are discussing?

"Sir?" his father asked.

"Nothing," Robby said.

"*Sir?*" Urgency now; bilked authority.

Robby felt the cold shudder running down his back and across his stomach.

"I said it was easy for him to talk," he repeated, holding his voice tightly in check, "he doesn't have to put on a—" his throat moved convulsively. "He doesn't have to face Benton."

"I fail to see . . ." His father left the question a challenge hanging in the air.

Robby looked up quickly and forced himself to stare straight into his father's eyes. The two of them looked at each other across the shop.

"Father," Robby said, tensely, "Benton has been in the Rangers, he's killed *thirteen* men—"

"I fail, sir, to see what this has to do with the situation at hand," Matthew Coles interrupted, his voice rising steadily to the end of the sentence.

No, you wouldn't!—the words tore at Robby's mind but he didn't have the strength to speak them aloud. He lowered his head and went back to the pistol, screwing on the walnut stock with tense, jerky movements.

"Sir, I'm beginning to wonder just what you're trying to say to me," Matthew Coles challenged, putting down the Winchester barrel with a determined thud.

Robby shook his head. "Nothing. I—"

"Sir?"

He shook his head again. "It's nothing, father." He felt his heart start pounding heavily.

"Sir, I demand an explanation!"

"I told you I'd do it!" Robby shouted, head jerked up so suddenly it made his neck muscles hurt. "Now leave me alone, will you!"

He couldn't seem to get the lump out of his throat. He kept swallowing futilely while his fingers shook helplessly on the Colt parts. He kept his eyes down, sensing the look his father was directing toward him.

Rigid control; that was the sound in his father's voice when he spoke again. The sort of rigid control that only a lifetime of practice could achieve; the sort of control based upon unyielding will.

"I have already accepted your statement to that effect," said Matthew Coles flatly. "It is no longer a question of doing or not doing, it is a question of time. Let me remind you, sir, that it is not only the honor of your intended bride that is at stake. Your own honor, too, as well as the honor of our family name, is at stake." Pause, a brief sound of metal clicking on metal.

"The next few days will determine the future of that honor," said Matthew Coles.

There was silence in the shop then, a heavy, ominous absence of sound, broken only occasionally by the slight clicking sounds of his father's work, the infrequent insect-like gasp of the small files. Robby Coles sat numbly, working on the pistol. Another chance was gone; he was in deeper yet. Every time he wanted to bring up the point of whether he should face Benton at all, his father or someone would make it clear that this point was not even in question, that the only thing that mattered now was—*when*?

Robby looked up cautiously at his father but Matthew Coles was studiedly absorbed in his work. For a long moment, Robby looked at the hard features that seemed chipped from granite—a deep blow for each eye, several harsh cuts for the large dominant nose, one long, unhesitating blow for the straight, unmoving mouth.

Then he looked back to his work. While he finished putting the Colt together with quick, agitated hand motions, he thought of Louisa being kept in the house because of what had happened.

The more he thought of it, the more it bothered him. She was his girl; he loved her and wanted to marry her. It *was* his job to defend her; nothing anyone said could change that, no argument could refute it.

And, after all, no one really wanted to see him die. His father hadn't raised him twenty-one years just to push him into being killed. O'Hara didn't have any reason to want Robby dead. All the people in town had no grudge against him. It was simply that they all expected him to defend the honor of his woman and Louisa was his woman. Either he stood up for her or he lost her for good and, with her, his self-respect. It was as simple as that; the thought struck him forcibly.

It was strange how this different approach to the matter seemed to pour courage, strength, into him. Louisa was his woman. He loved her and he'd fight for her.

That was his responsibility, his duty. Louisa was his intended bride, it was his job to—

The clicking of the trigger made Robby's flesh crawl.

He found himself suddenly, the assembled Colt held tensely in his right hand, his finger closed over the trigger.

With a spasmodic movement, he shoved the pistol away from himself and it banged down on the bench.

"Be careful!" Matthew Coles snapped.

Robby hardly heard his father. He sat shivering, his eyes fixed to the heavy, glinting form of the Colt, in his mind the hideous impression that, somehow, it was Benton's pistol and that he'd repaired it and put it together for Benton and it was in perfect working order now; it could fire, it could shoot a bullet.

It could kill.

Chapter Twelve

When Mrs. Angela DeWitt left the shop, Louisa came back to where her aunt sat writing in the ledger.

"Aunt Agatha?" she asked meekly, standing by the desk, her face drained with nervous worry.

Agatha Winston went on with her figures, her eyes shrewd and calculating behind the spectacles, her pen running crabbed hen-tracks of numbers across the lined page.

"Aunt Agatha?"

Agatha Winston's eyes closed shut. Beneath the mouse-fuzz of her mustache, her pinched mouth grew irked. Slowly, decisively, she put down the pen.

"What is it, Louisa?" she asked in the flinted tone that she conceived to be one of patience and forbearing.

Louisa stammered. "Aunt Agatha . . . *please*," she said. "May I—"

The jade eyes were hidden behind quickly lowered lids and Agatha Winston cut off the appearance of the world.

"You may *not* go home," she said, concisely. "There is much too much work to be done."

Louisa bit nervously at her finger, eyes pleading and lost.

"Heaven only knows," her aunt continued, "I ask little enough of your mother and yourself in return for the help I give you freely, with Christian affection." Agatha Winston sighed, head shaking once. "I'm tired, Louisa," she said. "I would like nothing better than to retire . . . and live on my small savings. But, for your mother's sake and for your own . . ." another sigh, ". . . I go on working. Asking *nothing* in return but a little help in the shop a few days out of the week." She fixed an accusing look upon her niece. "Is that so much to ask?" she said. "Is that so—stop that!"

Louisa jerked the moist, chewed knuckle from her lips and swallowed nervously.

"Is it, Louisa?" asked her aunt.

"No, Aunt Agatha, it . . . isn't that. I like to help you in the shop but . . ." She bit her lower lip and couldn't help the tear that wriggled from beneath her right eyelid and trickled down her cheek. "They all look at me so," she said, brokenly.

"And what would you like to do?" her aunt challenged. "Go home? Hide away as if you had something to be ashamed of?"

"No, Aunt Agatha, it isn't—"

"You might just as well confess your guilt as do that!"

Louisa's mouth twitched. "G-guilt?" she murmured, eyes wide and frightened.

"Yes," her aunt said. "Guilt. Is that what you want people to think; that you have something to be ashamed of?"

"*No*, Aunt Agath—"

"That's all there is to it," stated Agatha Winston firmly. "We have nothing to hide and we will not hide."

Louisa stared helplessly at her aunt.

"Let John Benton hide his face!" Agatha Winston said angrily. "Not us." She glared at Louisa, then picked up her pen. "Now . . . kindly take care of the shop until I finish my work."

Louisa still stood watching until her aunt looked

up again, dark eyes commanding. "Well?" said her
aunt.

Louisa turned and walked slowly down the length of
the counter. She stopped at the front of the shop and
looked out the window at the sunlit square.

She stared bleakly at the reversed letters painted on
the glass—MISS WINSTON'S LADIES APPAREL. Then her
eyes focused again beyond the letters and she looked at
the plank sidewalk, the dirt square, the shops across the
way. She looked a while at the motionless peppermint-
stick pole in front of Jesse Willmark's Barber Shop.
She thought of the look Jesse had given her when she
passed him that morning with her aunt. The memory
made her breath catch.

Then she saw a horseman ride by and look into the
shop and she turned away quickly, her cheeks coloring
embarrassedly. She hoped the man didn't see her blush.
The way he *looked* at her . . .

She stood with her back to the window a long time,
feeling a strange quiver in her body. She reached up
and brushed away a tear that dripped across her cheek.
Why did everybody look at her that way?

All during the last sale, Mrs. DeWitt had kept staring like that, always turning down her gaze a little too
late to hide the curious brightness in her eyes. Never
once did she say a word about the situation Louisa
knew she was thinking about. She talked about shifts
and stockings and corsets as if there were nothing else
on her mind. And, all the time, her eyes kept probing
up, then down, as if she were attempting to penetrate
Louisa's mind and ferret out its secrets.

All through the sale, Louisa had tried to smile, to repeat the things about the merchandise her aunt had
taught her. *Oh, yes this is what every woman back East
is wearing now. This is delicate but completely sturdy.
I think you'll find it will not bind or roll. This is the
best material of its type on the market.* Words repeated

in a nervous voice, when all the time she wanted to run away and hide.

Louisa glanced over her shoulder again and saw that there was no one in front of the shop. She turned back and looked out the window again. Far down in the south end of the square was the shop where Robby worked. Louisa looked in that direction.

All morning she'd been dreadfully afraid that Robby was going to come in and ask her if the story about Benton was really true. Every time she'd heard footsteps in the doorway or heard hoofbeats out front, her head had jerked up from whatever she was doing and she'd looked fearfully at the shop entrance, heart pounding suddenly. What would she tell him if he asked? How could she say she lied when Aunt Agatha was right there to hear the confession? She couldn't; she knew she couldn't.

He'd just have to stay away from her until everyone forgot about that silly story. They couldn't keep thinking about it forever. As long as they left her alone, it would be all right. She wished she could stay in the house until the story *was* forgotten. She didn't like people staring at her like that. It was terrible the way people gossiped and talked. All Louisa wanted to do was keep out of everyone's way until things were back to normal again.

Louisa started suddenly at the footsteps in the doorway and her body tightened apprehensively as she turned to see who it was.

Mrs. Alma Cartwright came waddling to the counter, hurriedly erasing from her plump face the curious look that had crossed it when she saw Louisa standing there.

"How are you, my dear?" she asked.

Louisa smiled faintly. "Well, thank you," she said.

"And your dear mother?" Mrs. Cartwright asked, sheep eyes looking quizzical.

Louisa swallowed and managed another smile. "Well," she said, "thank you, Mrs. Cartwright."

Mrs. Cartwright looked toward the back of the shop with forced casualness. "Oh, there's your aunt," she said, obviously disappointed that she wasn't alone with Louisa. "How *do*, Miss Winston."

Agatha Winston raised her head, smiled a merchant-to-buyer smile, nodded once, then returned grimly to her figures.

"May I . . . help you?" Louisa asked.

The gaze of her customer stabbed back at her. A smile was arranged on Mrs. Cartwright's puffy lips.

"I'd like to get a shirtwaist, my dear," she said. "Silk. For my girl. She's sixteen next week, you know."

"Oh," Louisa said, trying to sound pleasantly surprised.

She could almost feel the portly woman's eyes on her back as she fingered through the stack of shirtwaists in the drawer. A prickling sensation coursed her back, making her shudder. She drew in a quick breath and turned.

"No silk, Mrs. . . . . Cartwright," she finished weakly as the older woman forced the look of a buying customer on her face again.

"Oh. I'm sorry to hear that," said Mrs. Cartwright. "Well . . . perhaps . . . cotton?"

Louisa put the shirtwaist on the counter and stood there restively while the woman fingered it distractedly.

"This is the f-inest type sold in the market," Louisa said without expression. "You'll . . ."

She stopped as Mrs. Cartwright looked at her. The plump woman couldn't hide the look in her eyes. Aware of it, she stopped trying. She directed a furtive glance at Miss Winston, then smiled sadly.

"My dear girl," she said, behind the sympathy a probing inquisitiveness, "I've heard about this . . . terrible thing and I'm . . . I'm so shocked."

Louisa couldn't speak at first. She felt the heat licking up her cheeks again and had to press her lips together to keep them from shaking. She wanted to turn and run away but she knew she couldn't so she just stood there staring wordlessly, feeling Mrs. Cartwright's beady eyes on her, attempting to reflect compassion but conveying only a hungry curiosity.

"I'll ask my . . . my aunt to ah-show you another kind of—" she faltered, then turned away abruptly.

"But my dear, this is—"

Her skirt rustled noisily as she hurried up the counter, trying vainly to keep the hot tears from spilling any faster across her flushed cheeks.

"Aunt . . . A-Agatha," she sobbed.

Agatha Winston looked up suddenly, face a blank of consternation.

"What on earth . . ." she started, then stopped, her dark eyes staring at Louisa's anguished face.

"*Please*," Louisa begged, "I . . . I . . ." She couldn't finish.

Agatha Winston glanced up at the customer, then back at her trembling niece. "Go in the back room," she said. "*Quickly.*"

As Louisa stumbled away, cutting off a choking sob, Miss Winston moved in firm strides down the counter.

"I'm so sorry, Mrs. Cartwright," she said in a politely brittle voice. "Now what were we looking at?"

Mrs. Cartwright glanced back toward where Louisa was entering the back room.

"What did I say?" she asked. "My dear Miss Winston, I had no intention of—"

"It's nothing, nothing," Miss Winston assured hastily, plucking up the shirtwaist. "She's just a little upset. Is this what we're interested in today? Now this material is woven by the finest New England lo—"

She stopped talking and glared at Mrs. Cartwright who was looking toward the back of the shop again and acting upset.

"Mrs. Cartwright?" she asked.

The large woman looked at her, head shaking sadly. "Oh, my dear Miss Winston," she proclaimed, "my heart goes out to that poor girl."

Miss Winston stiffened. "I beg your pardon?" she said.

Again, Mrs. Cartwright glanced toward the back room. Then she leaned over the counter.

"Do you really think she should . . . wait counter when . . ." She gestured futilely. "Well . . ."

"Mrs. Cartwright, I'm afraid I do not know what you are talking about," Miss Winston enunciated slowly, torn between rising anger and the unquestioning demeanor she believed all customers merited.

Mrs. Cartwright looked unhappy. "Oh, my dear," she said in a sort of joyous agony at being involved in this moment. "We're all lambs in the Lord's flock. When one of us is led astray . . ."

She didn't finish. *Lambs?*—Miss Winston thought— led *astray?* Her eyes grew harder still behind her forgotten spectacles.

"Mrs. Cartwright, I'll thank you for an—"

"Oh, my dear Miss Winston. I feel nothing but sympathy for your poor dear niece. I would not for the world—"

"Mrs. Cartwright, what are you talking about?" Miss Winston demanded, putting aside, for the moment, the role of courteous vendor.

Mrs. Cartwright put her ample hand on the unresponsive fingers of Miss Winston.

"I know all about it," she whispered. "And it has made my heart go out to that poor, dear girl."

"What, exactly, do you know?" Miss Winston asked, face beginning to go slack now with the rising fear that she did not know everything.

Mrs. Cartwright looked around, looked back.

"About the baby," she whispered. "The—"

"What!" Miss Winston's virginal body lurched in shock, her fingers jerking out from beneath the moist warmth of Mrs. Cartwright's hand. "What are you talking about! Are you intimating that Louisa is—"

Her hands jerked into bone-jutting fists. "Oh!" she said, absolutely dumbfounded.

Mrs. Cartwright drew back in alarm. "What have I—?"

"I don't know where you heard this vicious gossip, Mrs. Cartwright!" Agatha Winston said, eyes burning with vengeful light, "but, let me end it now—right this very moment! It is not true, Mrs. Cartwright, it is not true at all! I'm shocked that you should believe such a terrible thing of my niece! Shocked, Mrs. Cartwright, *shocked*!"

"Oh, my dear Miss—"

"No. No. I don't want to hear anymore!" Miss Winston blinked as a wave of dizziness rushed over her. Her hands clutched at the counter edge. "Please leave," she muttered. "Please, leave my shop."

"*Oh* . . ." Miss Cartwright moaned, face a wrinkle of dismay.

Miss Winston turned away. "Please," she begged. "*Please.*"

When a shaken Miss Cartwright had retreated from the shop, an equally shaken Miss Agatha Winston found her unsteady way to the rear of the shop, throat constricted, eyes stark with premonition.

Louisa drew back in fright when she saw her aunt's face.

"Aunt Agatha," she whispered.

She gasped aloud as the clawing hand of her aunt clamped over her wrist.

"Tell me!" commanded Agatha Winston, her face terrible. "Is it true?"

Louisa shrank back. "What?" she asked, weakly.

"You had better tell me the truth!"

Louisa started sobbing again. "What?" she asked. "*What*, A-Aunt Agatha?"

Agatha Winston spoke slowly, teeth clenched. "*Are you with child?*"

Louisa gasped and stared blankly at her aunt, a heavy throbbing at her temples, legs shaking. She cried out suddenly as her aunt's hard fingers dug into her wrist.

"Answer me!" Agatha Winston cried, almost hysterically, her face mottled with an ugly rage.

"No!" Louisa sobbed. "No, I'm not. I'm not!"

A moment more did the two look at each other.

"Is that the truth?" Agatha Winston demanded tensely.

"Yes," Louisa insisted, tearfully. "*Yes.*"

Miss Winston released her niece's wrist and sank down weakly on a stool, chest heaving with breath, in her lap, her hands trembling impotently.

"Dear Lord," she muttered hoarsely. "*Dear Lord,*" her gaunt throat moving as she swallowed.

Louisa stood nearby, her body twitching with deep, unheard sobs. She wanted to run away but she was afraid to. Her mind swam with confused fears. With *child?*—she thought in a panic. Dear God, what was *happening*? She felt as if she were lost and helpless in a strange pit of terrors.

"Someone will pay for this," she heard her aunt muttering to herself. "Someone will *pay.*"

That was when they heard bootfalls in the shop entrance.

Louisa glanced over her shoulder to see who it was. Abruptly, she shrank back, eyes stark with fright, a gasp clutching at her throat. Instinctively, she drew to one side, away from the back room doorway.

Agatha Winston looked up, nerves about unstrung. "What is it now?" she hissed.

"It's . . . it—it's *him*!" Louisa whispered frantically.

Agatha Winston stood up quickly and stepped to the doorway.

Her thin nostrils flared, a calcification of outrage ran down her back. Hurriedly, she stepped away from the doorway.

"Stay back here," she ordered. "Don't move." Her agitated hands flew to her gray hair, to her skirt.

"Stay here," she said again, then moved out of the room and went behind the counter.

John Benton took off his hat as she approached him. He nodded his head politely and waited until she'd reached him.

"Afternoon, ma'm," he said then. "Are you Miss Winston?"

Her face was like stone. "I am," she said, controlling herself.

"My name is John Benton," he told her. "I—"

"I know your name," she said, coldly, wondering why she didn't erupt in his face. She would not admit nor even recognize the fact that she was afraid.

"You're Louisa Harper's aunt, aren't you?" Benton asked.

She said nothing. She swallowed the lump in her throat and stared at him, a trembling in her. She couldn't say anything but she wouldn't answer his questions anyway.

The politeness seemed to drift from Benton's face like a veil of smoke. His smile faded. "I'd like to speak to your niece," he said, softly.

"She is not here," said Agatha Winston.

Benton looked mildly confused. "What?" he said.

"My niece is not here," said Miss Winston slowly.

"Her mother said she was here," Benton answered.

Miss Winston's face lost color and she pressed together her trembling lips. Then she said, "Good day, Mister Benton."

He looked curiously at her hard, unyielding face.

Then he glanced toward the back of the shop. "Miss Winston," he said, "I believe I saw your niece when I came in."

Miss Winston shuddered with repressed fury. "She is not here," she said, tensely.

"Now, look here," Benton said. "What are you—"

"Good *day*, Mister Benton."

"Look here, Miss . . ." He gestured. ". . . Winston," he finished, remembering after a momentary lapse. "I came into town because there's some fool story goin' around that—"

"Will you leave my shop or do I have to call the sheriff?" Miss Winston shuddered, remembering suddenly that Sheriff Wilks was out of town for the week, taking a prisoner to the city.

Benton still didn't understand. "Look here, Miss Winston," he said, "I came here because—"

"Get out of here!" The control was suddenly gone; Miss Winston's face grew dark with rage again.

Benton didn't even change expression at her hysterical demand. He stood there looking incredulously at her while, outside, on the plank sidewalk, a passing couple stopped and listened.

"Look, I've had about enough of this—"

Benton stopped talking. Miss Agatha Winston was headed for the back of the shop, her dark skirts rustling angrily. She turned the counter edge and came stamping down the length of the shop.

At the door, she stopped and turned, ignoring the couple who moved on awkwardly, trying to act as if they'd seen nothing.

"Get out of here, you . . . !" The proper word escaped her. Miss Winston pointed one shaking finger out at the square.

A moment more, John Benton looked at her uncomprehendingly. Then he made a sound of complete bewilderment, slapped on his Stetson, and walked out of the shop.

Outside, he turned impulsively.

"Listen, will you tell your niece to—"

The banging of the slammed door cut off his words. John Benton stood there looking a little dazed as Miss Agatha Winston drew down the dark shades of her shop and shut him away.

Chapter Thirteen

Benton moved for his horse, not seeing the couple that stared at him, whispering between themselves. His face was tight with confusion as he swung up onto the saddle and drew Socks around. He started across the square for St. Virgil Street.

Then, halfway there, he pulled his mount around and headed for the small shop at the south end of the square. He'd try Robby then; maybe he could talk a little sense to a man. That woman—good God above! Benton shook his head amazedly, thinking about the way Miss Winston had acted. Maybe the Reverend was right, maybe this thing was getting a little bigger than it should. If it weren't, he would have ridden right back to the ranch and forgotten about it. But . . . well, he was here; he might as well try to end the thing if he could.

But with Robby, not with that Winston woman. Benton hissed slowly to himself. What a one *she* was.

In front of the shop, Benton reined up and dismounted. He tied Socks to the rack, then ducked under the bar and stepped up onto the plank sidewalk.

As he entered the small shop, it seemed to be empty. His gaze moved over the sun-speckled benches, the pistols and rifles hanging on the walls, the glass case on the front counter. That was a good-looking Colt there with its white-bone stock and shiny new metal. Benton felt the slight flexing in his fingers that came whenever he saw the well-made symmetry of the pistol he knew so well. It was so habitual, he hardly noticed it. His gaze drifted over the other pistols in the case.

He was looking at a Smith and Wesson .44 caliber six-shooter when Matthew Coles came out of the back room. Benton looked up at the sound of footsteps and met the glare of the older man.

Mr. Coles walked quickly to the counter. "State your business," he said curtly.

There was a slight wrinkling of skin around Benton's eyes as he looked inquisitively at Matthew Coles.

"Is your son here?" he asked.

"He is not."

Benton met the older man's stony look without change of expression. "Where can I find him?" he asked.

Matthew Coles was silent.

"I said—where can I find your son?" Benton repeated as if he hadn't noticed the slight.

"When the time comes," said Matthew Coles, "he will find you."

"Now, wait a minute," Benton said, the tanned skin tensing across his cheek bones. "Let's get this straight. This fool story about me and—"

"I am not interested in stories," Matthew Coles declared.

Benton took a deep, controlling breath. "I think you better be interested in this one," he said.

Mr. Coles said nothing.

"Listen, Coles, this thing isn't funny anymore."

"It is, decidedly, not funny," said Matthew Coles, his gaze dropping for a searching instant to John Benton's left hip, then raising as instantly, assured. "You have presumed too much on your popularity, Mister Benton. That was a mistake."

"If you're talkin' about that girl, you're all wrong," Benton said. "I never even *spoke* to her since I been in Kellville."

The thinnest hint of a smile played at the corners of Matthew Coles' mouth. "You don't have to come explaining to me," he said.

Benton strained forward a moment, body tensed, something in his eyes making Matthew Coles draw back, slack-faced.

Benton swallowed, controlling himself with difficulty.

"Where's your son?" he asked, tensely. "I want to see him."

"He does not wish to see you," Coles said.

Repressed anger seemed to ripple beneath the surface of Benton's face. "Listen, Coles," he said, "I came into town to end this fool story, not to be pushed around."

"I'm sure you didn't," said Matthew Coles, stiffly. "However, since you are no longer man enough to wear a gun you cannot very well command respect, can you?"

Again the tightening of Benton's muscles; at his sides, his fingers twitching.

"You're an old man," he said, softly. "But don't overplay it, Coles, don't overplay it."

Mindless rage flared up lividly in Matthew Coles' face. "Get out of my shop!" he ordered.

"My pleasure," Benton said, turning on his heel and starting for the door.

"You will hear from us, sir!" Coles shouted after him.

"I'm sure I will," Benton said, without looking back.

Then, at the door, he turned.

"Now listen to me, old man," he said, warningly. "Stop pushing this damn thing. If you don't, somebody's goin' to get hurt, understand? You've got a good kid. Don't push him into somethin' he's not up to. I've got no grudge against Robby and he's got no reason to hold any grudge against me. Understand? None at all. Tell him that." Benton's face hardened in an instant. "And *stay away*!"

The look was gone as quickly as it came. "I don't want trouble from anyone, Coles," Benton said. "Not from anyone."

Matthew Coles stood shaking with wordless rage behind the counter, staring at Benton's back as he went out of the shop, stepped off the plank walk, and untied his horse.

For a long time he stood there in the silence of the shop, trembling with impotent fury, his shallow chest rising and falling strainedly.

Then he went to the back of his shop and looked through the collection of new pistols for the one his son would use to kill John Benton.

Chapter Fourteen

"**W**hy do you *think* he left the Rangers?" Jesse Willmark challenged his suds-faced customer. " 'Cause he got *tired* of it? No. 'Cause he was too old? No. I'll tell you why." He leaned forward, gesturing with the sun-reflecting razor. "Because he turned yella, that's why."

"Couldn't say," the customer muttered.

"Look, ya remember the time—'bout a year or so ago, I guess it was—when they was gettin' up a posse to chase Tom Labine? You remember that?" Jesse asked, setting up his coup de grace.

"Yeah. What about it?"

"I'll tell you what about it," Jesse broke in intently. "They asked Benton t'help them. Sheriff Wilks don't know a dang thing about trailin' or 'bout anythin' for that matter. So they asked Mister John Benton t'help them out. You think he would? The hell he would! Can't do it, he says, cut me out. *Why*? Why wouldn't he help out his neighbors?"

"Maybe he didn't want to," the customer suggested.

"Hell, man," Jesse said, "I'll tell ya why he wouldn't do it." He raked the razor across the man's soap-stubbled cheek with a practiced gesture. "He was yella, that's why. He didn't have the guts to ride another posse. His nerves is gone and that's a fact."

"Could be," the customer said.

Jesse wiped the beard-flecked lather off his razor. He rubbed his pudgy fingers over the customer's cheek, rubbing in the warm soap.

"I'll tell ya somethin' else," he said, eyes narrowing. "It happens to all o' them. I don't know how—or why—but one day—" he snapped his fingers, "like that—they're yella."

He started shaving again. "They go on year after year shootin' 'em down like sittin' ducks," he said, "then, one day—*bang*—they turn yella; they get scared o' their own shadda. It's nerves what it is. Ain't no man alive can go on like that year after year without losin' his nerve."

He nodded grimly.

"And that's what happened to Benton," he said. "Mind, I ain't takin' nothin' away from the man. He was a big lawman in his day, brave as they come, quick on the draw. Course he never was as big as they painted him but—" he shrugged, "—he was a good lawman. But that don't mean he can't turn yella. That don't mean he didn't. He did—and that's a fact."

He shaved away beard from the customer's throat.

"Hard to say," the customer said, looking at the paint-flaked ceiling.

"All right," Jesse said, wiping off the razor edge again. "If he's still brave as he was, why don't he wear a gun, answer me that?"

The customer said he didn't know.

"Because he's *scared* to pack one!" Jesse exclaimed as if it were a great truth he had to convey. "No man goes around without a gun less'n he's too scared to use it. Ain't that true?"

The customer shrugged. "It's a point," he conceded.

"Sure as hell is a point!" Jesse said. "Benton don't pack no gun 'cause he's scared to back hisself up with hot lead."

The customer grunted, then sat up as Jesse adjusted the head rest.

"Then to go and do what he done," Jesse said, shaking his head. "Him a married man and all."

The customer could see the front door in the mirror.

"Jesse," he said, softly.

"I'll tell ya, it sure surprised the hell outta me," Jesse said, stropping the razor. "It's a bad thing when a man starts goin' down."

"Jesse." A warning; but too soft. The customer sat stiffly in the chair, trying not to look at the mirror.

"Specially a man like Benton," said Jesse. "Him bein' such a big lawdog and all. First he yellas out, then he starts playin' around with—"

"*Jesse.*"

Jesse broke off and looked at the customer. "What is—?" he started to ask, then saw how the man was looking into the mirror. His throat tightened abruptly as he glanced up and saw the reflection of John Benton, tall and grim-faced, standing in the doorway.

Jesse didn't dare turn. He stood there, staring helplessly into the mirror, his throat moving as he tried to swallow fear.

"I'd keep my mouth shut unless I knew what I was talkin' about," Benton said coldly.

Then he turned and was gone and a white-faced Jesse whirled to exclaim, "Honest, Mister Benton, I didn't—!"

But Benton was gone. Jesse hurried to the doorway, razor in shaking hand, and watched Benton mount his horse.

Then he turned back hurriedly to his customer, a look of uncontrollable dread on his face.

"Jesus," he said, hollowly. "You don't think he'll do anything to me, do you?"

The customer looked blandly at the slack-faced barber in the mirror.

"You don't think he'll come after me, do you?" Jesse asked, getting weaker. "Do you?"

The barest suggestion of a smile. "How can he?" the customer asked. "He's yella."

Chapter Fifteen

David James O'Hara could be a very impressive young bully when he tried. His face was lean and hard beneath a short crop of reddish hair. He moved with a catlike swiftness, swaggered convincingly, swore and gambled, wore a Colt .44 low on his hip, thonged to his leg, and spoke deprecatingly of every gunman who ever rode within a hundred miles of Kellville.

There had been a few shootings in the little town but, somehow, Dave O'Hara was never around when they occurred. He was twenty-three years old and still believed in his own courage because it had never been tried. The one man who had challenged O'Hara had left town without fighting and thus strongly increased O'Hara's opinion of himself.

It was about two-thirty in the afternoon. O'Hara was sitting at a back table in the Zorilla talking to Joe Sutton who was losing at cards and arguing.

"You kiddin', Sutton?" O'Hara said, putting down his card with a slap. "He's cold-footed. If he ain't scared o' Robby, why don't he wear a gun?"

Sutton swallowed. "Well, why don't he?" O'Hara challenged.

"He wouldn't say," Sutton answered.

"Y'mean you asked him?" O'Hara looked up in surprise from his hand.

"Yeah," said Joe Sutton, "I ast him yestiday mornin' but—"

"But he wouldn't tell ya," O'Hara finished. "Course he wouldn't tell ya. Think a man's gonna come right out and admit he's yella? Play your card."

Sutton licked his lips and looked worriedly at his hand, deeply troubled by the impending crumble of faith.

"Well, you should've seen him," he said then, looking up. "You should've seen him do the border roll and . . . and the shift. You know, tossin' his iron from one hand to the other. It was so fast I couldn't hardly see it." He swallowed at O'Hara's unresponsive stare. "That's how fast it was," he repeated weakly.

"So what does that mean?" O'Hara asked. "Anybody can do tricks with a gun when they's no one facin' 'em. I'd like t'see him do gun tricks with another guy throwin' down on him."

Sutton swallowed. "Well . . ." he said but that was all. He swallowed again and played the wrong card.

"Him and that cocklebur outfit o' his," O'Hara muttered. "He's no better'n a sheep herder." His fingers tightened on the dog-eared cards. "Livin' on his repitation, that's what he's tryin' t'do. Thinks he can play around with any girl he wants cause he has a repitation. Well, Robby'll show 'im."

Joe Sutton shook his head. "Y'think he'll really go after Benton?" he asked.

O'Hara pointed a finger at Sutton. "You bet ya damn life he will," he said. "Then we'll see how good ol' lawdog Benton is. Bet he won't even put on a gun!"

"What else could he do?" Sutton asked, faintly.

"Hide, most likely," O'Hara said. "Hide on his ranch like a yella hound."

Sutton looked pained. Then he looked up and said, "Uh-oh. Watch out."

O'Hara looked toward the doors which were just swinging shut behind John Benton's tall form.

"Whataya mean, watch out?" he said, a little more loudly than he'd intended. "I ain't afraid o' him."

Benton glanced toward them, then walked to the bar, his face hard with anger.

"Pat," he greeted the bartender flatly as the older man came up to him.

"The usual, Mister Benton?"

"Yeah."

Benton could hear the voice of O'Hara in back saying something about a shirt-tail outfit as he watched the amber whiskey being poured.

"What's goin' on around here, Pat?" he asked then, looking up.

"You mean about Robby and—"

"Yeah. What the hell's the matter with everybody? One day and it seems like half the town's out to get me."

"Well, now," Pat said casually, "little folks always like to try'n topple the big ones, it seems. It's human nature."

Benton smiled ruefully. "I'm just a little feller, Pat," he said. "No reason for anyone to—"

Abruptly, he stopped talking and glanced again toward the back table, hearing the words *cold-footed* spoken loudly. He squinted a little at the young man sitting in the shadows. He saw young Joe Sutton's face twitch in the repression of a smile, then he looked back at the bar. He picked up the glass and took a swallow.

"Who's that in the black shirt?" he asked, quietly.

"Dave O'Hara," Pat told him.

"Don't know him." Benton drank some more.

"Local loudmouth," Pat said. "He don't amount to nothin'."

Benton grunted, then put down his glass. "Pat?" he said.

"What's that, Mister Benton?"

Benton took a deep breath and let it out slowly.

"What's happening around here, Pat? What's the latest on this . . ." he gestured vaguely with one hand, ". . . this thing?"

Pat made a sound of wry amusement. "You wouldn't believe it," he said.

Benton thought about the last half hour he'd spent. He thought about Miss Agatha Winston, Mr. Matthew Coles, Jesse Willmark.

"I'd believe it," he said.

"More?" Pat asked and Benton nodded, pushing the glass forward.

Pat looked up from the bottle. "The talk is," he said, "that Robby Coles is gonna come after ya."

Benton looked at him blankly. "Yeah?" he said as if he expected clarification. Then, suddenly, his mouth opened. "You don't—" He put down the glass. "You don't mean with a gun?" he asked, incredulously.

Pat shrugged. "That's the talk," he said.

Benton started to say something, then stopped and stared at Pat.

"That's crazy," he said then. "He's fryin' size, for God's sake!"

Pat said nothing. In the silence, they heard O'Hara say, "Come on, let's belly up," and then the scraping back of chair legs and the irregular thump of two pairs of boots across the saloon floor. Benton paid no attention. He kept staring at Pat, his expression still one of disbelief.

"My God," he murmured. "I never thought for a minute that . . ." Slowly, he shook his head. "But that's crazy," he said. "Would . . . would he be fool enough to do that?"

Pat shrugged again. "Couldn't say, Mister Benton," he said. "But if enough people push him . . ." He didn't finish but moved up the bar to where O'Hara and Sutton stood.

"So that's what his old man meant," Benton murmured to himself, remembering Matthew Coles' words. "My God, I never . . ."

He fingered at the glass restlessly, his face a mask of worried concentration reflected back to him in the big mirror. He shook his head concernedly.

He didn't hear the deprecating chuckle that O'Hara made. The first thing he did hear vaguely was something that sounded like, "What're ya *scared* of? *He* ain't got no gun on." But he wasn't sure that's what it was as he glanced down the bar at the two young men. John Benton wasn't used to having people discuss him slightingly when he was around and he couldn't quite believe that such a thing was happening now.

He saw the movement of Sutton's throat and how he stared into his drink suddenly. Then the insulting blue eyes of O'Hara met Benton's. Benton looked back to his drink immediately. There were enough things to worry about already. He took a deep breath and drank some of the whiskey. It threaded its hot way down his throat. Good God, what *now*? Bond was right, the thing was serious. But how did it get that way so quick? Everybody must really believe that he spoke to Louisa Harper. My God, what did they think he *said* to her? The barber talked about "playing around"; is that what they thought he was trying to do with the Harper girl?

Benton's broad chest rose quickly as he drew in a worried breath. It was bad, it was really bad. This was the first time anything even remotely like it had happened in his—

The chuckling again; unmistakable. Benton heard the words *cold-footed* again, obviously spoken, and something jerked in his stomach muscles. He looked over quickly and saw O'Hara looking at him again. Benton felt the muscles drawing in along his arms, the rising flutter of pulse beat in his wrists. Without a sound, he put down his glass, drew his boot from the rail, and started walking along the bar.

Sutton stepped back as he approached. A failing smile faltered on the young man's lips as he watched Benton with his dark, intent eyes.

Benton stopped a few feet from O'Hara, his arms hanging loosely at his sides.

"You got somethin' to say to me?" he asked, quietly.

A look of instinctive fear paled O'Hara's face. He pushed it away and forced back his habitual expression of arrogant assurance. But, when he spoke, the slight trembling of his voice belied the look.

"No," he said. "I ain't got nothin' t'say to you."

Benton's mouth tightened a little.

"If you do," he said, "say it to me, not to your friend here."

Sutton opened his mouth as if to assure Benton that O'Hara wasn't his friend but he said nothing.

"If I got anything to say, I'll say it," O'Hara replied trying to look belligerent.

"Good," Benton said. "That's fine."

Then he saw the slight dipping of O'Hara's gaze.

"No, I don't have a gun on," he said abruptly. "But don't let that bother you." He could feel the anger rising inside him like a fire, creeping along his arteries and veins. His temper was going; he was getting sick and tired of people looking to see if he was armed before they said what they really meant.

"I don't talk to no one who—" O'Hara hesitated momentarily, looking for words a little less insulting, "who don't wear no gun," he finished, realizing then that he couldn't afford to hesitate.

"Listen, *flannel-mouth*," Benton said, "I've had about enough from—"

"Don't call me that!" O'Hara flared up impulsively, his voice rising shrilly. "God damn it, I'll—"

"You'll what!" Benton snapped in a sudden burst of rage. "What!"

O'Hara hesitated a split second, then lunged down for his pistol. Benton's arm shot out.

"*Hold it!*"

They both twitched into immobility and looked across the bar to where Pat had a big army pistol aimed at O'Hara's chest.

"Put it away, boy," Pat ordered. "Would ya draw on an un-armed man?"

The look of sudden surprise on O'Hara's face was changed to one of frustrated rage.

"Sure!" he said, loudly. "Sure! Get a bardog to save ya! You're too yella t'save yourself!"

His voice shook thinly as he raged and, hearing it, the tension seemed to drain off inside Benton. For a moment, he looked at O'Hara without expression. Then a thin smile relaxed his mouth, a brief chuckle sounded in his chest.

"If you ever see me with a gun on," he said, amusedly, "you just say that again."

"I'll never see ya with a gun on!" O'Hara went on, furious at the lost advantage. "You ain't got the guts t'put a gun on!"

Benton turned away casually.

"Robby Coles'll kill ya!" O'Hara said loudly. "He'll *kill* ya, Benton!"

Benton turned back quickly, face tight. "Shut your mouth, boy," he said in quiet menace, "or, by God, I'll belt on a gun right now; is that what you want?"

O'Hara had the self-preserving sense to glare speechlessly at Benton until the tall man had turned away. Joe Sutton watched Benton walk back to where his glass was.

"Thanks Pat," Benton said quietly. "He might've killed me."

"He might've at that," Pat said, pouring.

Benton threw down the new drink. "Well, I'm goin' back to the ranch," he said clearly. "I've had enough for one day."

"What about . . . ?" Pat didn't finish.

"Who, Robby?" Benton shrugged and made a

disgusted sound. "The hell with it," he said quietly. "I've done all I'm goin' to do for one day. I'll just stay on my spread till the damn thing blows over. One thing sure." He put down the glass with a gesture of finality. "Robby's not goin' to come after me with a gun. You know that."

Pat said no more but he looked dubious.

When the swinging doors had shut behind Benton, O'Hara looked up.

"Lucky for him he's got a bardog watchin' over him."

"Lucky for you, too," Pat told him.

"But he said—" Joe Sutton started.

"Sure," O'Hara said, bitterly. "Sure, he said he'd belt on a gun. What gun? Did he have one with him? Was he gonna make one outta the air?"

"Oh, shut up, O'Hara," Pat said casually and the young man glared at him, tight mouth trembling.

Sutton looked into his foamy beer. He wasn't sure. He didn't want to believe O'Hara, he wanted to believe that Benton wasn't afraid of anything. And yet O'Hara was right, Benton *didn't* have a gun and it was easy to talk when you had nothing to force you to back yourself up with. And, besides, Benton said he was going back to the ranch. If Robby Coles was out to get him, why did Benton go back to his ranch? And why didn't he wear a gun?

Joe Sutton shook his very young head. He didn't understand.

Chapter Sixteen

Late afternoon. Miss Agatha Winston stalked again, a clicking of dark heels, a snapping rustle of skirt. But where the previous day it had been Davis Street, today it was Armitas. Where the previous day she had been headed, stiff-legged and shocked, for the house of her sister, this day she was, infuriated and vengeance-bound, headed for the house of Matthew Coles. She was still in black, however, she still carried, in one gaunt-handed grip, her black umbrella and, in her eyes, there still burned the fire of inflexible outrage.

At the gate which led to the Coleses' house, Miss Winston paused not a jot but unlatched, shoved, stepped in, and slammed behind. Beneath her marching heels, the gravel crunched and flinched aside, the porch steps echoed with a wooden hollowness, the welcome mat was crushed. Miss Agatha Winston grasped the heavy knocker and hurled it against the thick-paneled door, then stood stiffly in the almost twilight air, waiting for acknowledgment.

A moment passed. Then, inside, a labored trudging of footsteps sounded. The door was drawn open slowly and the care- and time-worn face of Mrs. Coles appeared.

"Miss Winston," she said, her tone caught between polite surprise and apprehension.

"Good afternoon," Miss Winston announced. "Is Mister Coles at home?"

"Why . . . no, he's still at his shop."

Grayish lips pursed irritably. "Is your older son at home?" Miss Winston asked.

"Why, no, Robby is at his father's shop too," said Mrs. Coles.

"Do you expect them home soon?"

Jane Coles swallowed gingerly. "Why . . . yes, they should be home . . . very soon."

"I see. I'd like to wait if you don't mind," said Miss Agatha Winston.

"Oh." Mrs. Coles smiled faintly. "Of course," she said and then, after a moment's hesitation, stepped aside. "Won't you . . . come in, Miss Winston?"

"Thank you." The black-garbed woman entered and stopped in the center of the hallway rug.

"Won't you . . . come into the sitting room?" Jane Coles invited. "They'll be home soon now."

Miss Winston nodded once and walked into the sitting room followed by Mrs. Coles, who walked on the rug as if it were a carpet of eggs.

"Please," said Jane Coles in her nearly inaudible voice, "sit down, Miss Winston."

Miss Winston, with one slowly modulated dip, settled down on the couch edge and, drawing her umbrella to the tip of her black shoes, leaned her hands upon the handle.

Mrs. Coles stood near the hall door, a smile faltering on her lips. She knew exactly what Miss Winston was there for but she could not, for a moment, speak of it. As a result, she stood quietly, a sick churning in her stomach as she tried to smile at the forbidding face of the other woman.

"Would you . . . care for a cup of tea?" she asked, suddenly, embarrassed by the silence.

"No, thank you," said Miss Winston.

Mrs. Coles stood there, looking awkward.

"Please," Miss Winston said, finally, "don't feel obligated. If you have work to do, please do it. I'll be perfectly all right here."

"Oh." A pleasant smile strained for a moment on the pale-rose features of Matthew Coles' defeated wife. "All right." She swallowed. "They . . . should be home very soon," she assured.

"Yes," said Miss Winston. "Thank you. I'll just wait here."

"All right." Mrs. Coles backed off, smiling, her insides tied in great knots of dreading. "I'll . . . get back to my . . . my work then," she said. Another smile, another almost imperceptible movement of her throat. "If you . . . want anything," she said, "I'll . . . I'll be in the kitchen."

Miss Winston nodded, not having smiled once since she came to the door. She watched the small woman turn and fade out of the room and heard the weary trudge of Mrs. Coles' feet moving down the hall and then the swinging open and shutting of the kitchen door.

She still sat rigidly as before in the silence of the room, her eyes straight ahead, focused only on the resolution of her inner thoughts.

In the hall, the brass-plated pendulum swung in slow, measured arcs and the ticking of the clock tapped metallically at the air. Miss Winston shifted a trifle on the edge of the horsehair couch, her nostrils dilating slightly with an indrawn breath. Her eyes focused a moment on the room and she saw, across from her, a gold-framed family photograph hanging on the wall.

There was Matthew Coles, dominating his family in light and shadow as in actuality—standing, dark-suited, face a Caesar-like cast, the hand he held on the shoulder of his seated wife appearing less as an encouragement of love than as a force pinning her down.

Mrs. Coles sat in stolid patience, on her emotionless

face only hints of the charm and beauty that had once been hers. Next to her sat the gangly, freckle-spotted Jimmy Coles, his discomfort at being stuffed into low-neck clothes clearly visible.

And, behind him, stood Robby, his face sober and youthfully good-looking, both hands resting on the back of his younger brother's chair.

Miss Winston's eyes shifted up again to the imperious challenge of Matthew Coles' face. Fine looking man, she thought, *fine; decent.* Her throat moved and she made haste to ignore the rising flutter of something unwanted by her virginal system. She drew in a tense breath and stared into her thoughts again, stirring up the mud-thick waters of righteous anger.

She was still sitting like that when the two horses came clopping up the alleyway, when the back door opened and shut and the commanding voice of Matthew Coles sounded in the house.

Quiet talking in the kitchen. Then, footsteps. Miss Winston looked up as Mr. Coles crossed the room, hand extended.

"Miss Winston," he said gravely and they shook cold hands. Behind, in the hallway, Robby lingered hesitantly.

"Good afternoon, Mister Coles," Agatha Winston said. Their hands parted.

"Mrs. Coles said that you wish to speak to me."

"To you *and* your son," Miss Winston amended.

Mr. Coles looked into the coal-dark eyes of Miss Agatha Winston and saw a message of rock-like determination there. Then he turned quickly and, without a word, motioned in his son.

Robby entered restively, trying to smile at Miss Winston but failing. He knew why she was there and the thought terrified him.

"Good afternoon . . . Miss Winston," he said, his voice cracking.

She nodded once, recognizing his presence.

"May we sit?" Mr. Coles asked and Miss Winston gestured with one hand. "Please," she said.

Matthew Coles and his son sat down.

"Now," said Mr. Coles, "I believe I know why you're here."

"I'm glad," Miss Winston said, with one curt nod. "I'm glad someone in this town recognizes the gravity of this ugly situation." She was thinking with particular deprecation of the Reverend Omar Bond.

"We have recognized it, Miss Winston," Matthew Coles assured her. "Believe me, ma'm."

Robby sat on the chair, feeling numb, a cold and ceaseless sinking in his stomach. No, he thought. No. It was all he could think. No. No.

"Then I think it's time a course of action was settled upon," said Miss Winston. "This cannot be allowed to go on any further."

"I agree with you," said Matthew Coles. "I agree with you entirely." He nodded grimly, thinking that here was a woman who spoke his language, who thought as a woman *should* think—with clarity, with decision.

"Well, then . . ." said Miss Winston.

"My son, Robert," said Mr. Coles, "realizing that it is his responsibility as your niece's intended husband, has agreed to defend her honor."

Miss Winston nodded in agreement.

"And," Matthew Coles went on, "to use force against Benton unless a complete and public apology is made."

Robby bit his lip. "But, I—" he started, too weakly to be heard. He leaned forward, the blood pounding in his head. He hadn't agreed to anything like that. He watched the two of them with sick eyes as they planned the use of his life.

"Apology?" said Miss Winston with a coldly withdrawn tone.

"Well," Mr. Coles explained, "I am not a man to shirk the truth, ma'm. But neither am I a man to advocate violence unless it is absolutely necessary. Mister

Benton was in my shop today disclaiming any responsibility in this matter."

Miss Winston looked shocked. "But you didn't believe him?" she said, tensely.

"Naturally not," Matthew Coles assured her. "However . . . we must allow for all possibilities other than violence, ma'm. I believe John Benton to be guilty as charged. But, if he is willing, before the public eye, to confess his guilt and repent, I . . . see no reason why violence should not be avoided."

Matthew Coles leaned back, thinking himself a quite reasonable and impartial man.

"But if he said he didn't do it," Robby suddenly broke in, "he's not going to apologize!" His voice was nervously excited as he spoke. His hands were cold and shaking in his lap.

"Sir," Matthew Coles declared firmly, offended at this outburst as reflecting on his parenthood, "the conditions as stated are unchangeable. Either Benton admits his guilt and repents . . . or violence must, unavoidably, be used upon him."

Robby felt himself shake as a wave of nausea swept over him. I'm not going to die!—the anguished thought cut through his brain—I'm *not*!

"One moment," Miss Winston started heatedly, "all this talk of admission and, and of apology is no longer reasonable. This afternoon I took my niece home in a near-hysterical state. She will be compelled to remain there until this terrible thing is settled. Not by her mother, not by me but by gossip! She's been driven from the streets by scorn!"

Matthew Coles looked indignant and shocked.

"In my shop this very afternoon," Miss Winston went on, furiously, "a customer—I won't mention her name—asked me—bold as you please!—if it were true that Louisa was—" she swallowed reticence, withdrawal, ingrained shame of all things physical, "—was with child!" she finished, her voice a whisper of passionate outrage.

Matthew Coles stiffened as though someone had struck him violently across the face. Robby looked suddenly blank.

There was shocked silence a moment, then the low, teeth-clenched voice of Matthew Coles rolling out slowly.

"Naturally," he said, "this puts an entirely new aspect on the situation."

"But . . . but Louisa never said that—" Robby started.

"It no longer matters what Louisa said!" Agatha Winston cried out vehemently. "What matters is that her reputation and the reputation of our entire family is being dragged through the mud!"

Robby flinched at her angry words and stared at Miss Winston speechlessly.

"Unless you stand up for my niece, she'll never be able to lift her head in Kellville again! She will be shamed, her mother will be shamed, and I'll be shamed!" Miss Winston's voice broke and she began sobbing dryly, hoarsely.

"My dear Miss Winston," Matthew Coles said quickly, jumping up from his chair, a fiercely accusing glare thrown at his son.

Miss Winston fought for control, hastily and ashamedly brushing away the hot tears that sprang from her eyes.

"We're shamed, *shamed*!" she sobbed miserably.

From where he sat, motionless and numb, Robby could see the whitened pulsing at his father's jaw, the tense set of his mouth. He looked down at the weeping Miss Winston for a moment. Then, before his father could say a word or look toward him, Robby stood with one wooden motion. He couldn't feel his hands or his feet, only the blood pounding so hard at his temples that he thought his veins would burst and spatter blood across his face.

He didn't know if it was courage or cold, drained terror. But his mind suddenly recognized the situation in all its clarity—Louisa driven into hiding, the town leering at her, picking at her reputation with insulting fingers.

"Don't cry, Miss Winston," he heard a strange, unnatural voice say in his throat.

Miss Agatha Winston looked up at the grim-faced young man and it seemed for a moment to Robby as if both she and his father were old and helpless and that it was up to him alone to settle the matter.

"Louisa will be defended," he heard the words go on as though he stood apart, listening. "Her honor will be defended. I'll stand up for her."

"*When*?" his father asked and it seemed a perfectly reasonable question in that moment, a question spoken from necessity.

"Tomorrow," Robby said. "Tomorrow I will."

His brain seemed to be hanging in a great, icy emptiness, like some crystalline machine suspended in a winter's night, bodiless—clicking and moving of itself, divorced from all fear and trepidation. There was a responsibility to be assumed, nothing else mattered. Manhood required it and he must live or fall by the demand. Tomorrow he would fight John Benton in the only way it could be done.

Robby Coles knew his father was shaking his hand strongly but he didn't feel it and he hardly saw it.

Chapter Seventeen

"**N**o, sir," John Benton said over the supper table that night, "I admit I'm still a tenderfoot when it comes to cattle ranchin' but one thing I do know; you're not goin' to get as strong a cowhorse lettin' 'em graze. Feed 'em grain; they earn it. They're a lot better workers for it."

Lew Goodwill shrugged his thick shoulders. "Well, I guess that's up to you, boss," he said. "Most outfits I rode with, though, let their hosses graze."

Benton took a drink of his hot coffee, then put down the cup. "No, grain makes harder muscles," he said. "Gives 'em more endurance, I know that for a fact."

Julia brought more biscuits to the table and sat back down to her supper without a word. She probed listlessly at her meat, the fork held apathetically in her fingers.

Benton noticed how she toyed with her food and reached across the broad table to put his hand on hers. She looked up with a faint smile.

"Honey, stop worryin'," he told her. "Nothin's goin' to happen."

Her smile was unconvincing. "I hope so," she said.

Merv Linken made a wry face as he chewed his beef. "Ma'm, you ain't got nothin' to fret about. Robby Coles ain't bucklin' on no iron against yore husband." He made a mildly scoffing sound. "That'd be like tryin' t'scratch his ear with his elbow."

Julia tried to appear reassured but was unable to manage it.

"Saw the Reverend ridin' out o' here, this mawnin'," Lew Goodwill said, looking up from his food. "What'd he want?"

Benton always wanted his men to feel as if they were part of the family and, as a result, there were few secrets among them.

"Yeah, what'd that ol' sin-buster want, anyway?" Merv asked, his leathery face deadpan, his light blue eyes fixed on Julia.

"Merv, you stop that," Julia scolded and the deadpan changed to cheerful grinning. Julia tried not to smile back but couldn't keep from it.

"You're a terrible man, Merv Linken," she said, the corners of her mouth forcing down the smile. "There's no hope for you."

"He came out to say I should ride into town and clear it all up," Benton told Lew Goodwill when his wife had finished. "You know the rest."

Lew shook his heavy head. "Darndest thing," he said, "makin' such a fuss over nothin'."

"It's something to them," Benton said. "They're usin' both barrels on me."

"Well . . ." Julia looked worried again. "Well, shouldn't we go in and try to settle it then? We could have the Reverend get everyone together in his house and . . ." She hesitated. ". . . well, clear it up," she finished.

"Honey, I told ya the way they all acted," John told her. "They just about threw me outta town. Even the barber's spreadin' lies about me." He exhaled disgustedly. "Then when that kid, that—what's his name?—O'Hara tried to fill his hand on me . . ." He shook his head grimly. "I've had enough, Julia. I'll just stay out here on the ranch and let 'em all stew in their own juice till they cook themselves."

"But, what if Robby comes after you?"

"Ma." John looked patiently at his wife. "Can you feature that? Can you feature that little feller puttin' on a gun and comin' after me?"

Julia looked down at her plate. "You know what his father is like," she said, quietly. "You know what Mr. Coles said."

"He was riled," Benton said, grinning. "I called him an old man and that bristled him." The two other men chuckled. "No, Coles isn't goin' to push his own boy into the grave," Benton finished.

"I . . . suppose."

Julia still played with her supper, finally putting down the fork altogether and drinking some coffee. Then she got up and brought an apple pie to the table and cut thick slices of it for the three men.

While she cleaned the supper scraps onto the hound dog's plate, she heard the three men talking about bits. None of them sounded concerned, least of all her husband. And Benton wasn't the type of man who hid his worries very effectively.

Julia thought to herself. John was probably right. There was a lot of fuss, yes, but Robby Coles knew John's reputation and couldn't possibly consider trying to fight him with a . . .

But what if he *did*, what if he was *forced* to? Julia stood by the pump, staring across the kitchen at her husband. What if Robby *did* come after him?

Julia Benton closed her eyes suddenly and did the only thing she could think of at the moment. She prayed; but it wasn't out of fear for her husband's life, it was something else.

Chapter Eighteen

It was dark in the room, silent. Out in the breeze-less night, crickets rasped like a thousand files grating on metal. A block away, she heard the muffled trotting of a horse as someone rode home late from town. The hoofbeats faded, disappeared, and the curtain of dark silence settled once again over the street, the house, the room in which she lay, sleep-less, on her bed.

In the back bedroom, in the bed so painfully large for her, her mother dozed fitfully, mumbling and whimpering in her sleep. Her husband had been dead eight years now but Elizabeth Harper still slept in the outsize four-poster, cold, restless, and lonely. She had never been quite the same since the funeral. They had, almost literally, buried her in the cemetery with her husband.

At least her spirit was there in the ground with his resting bones. Since his death, she had never been quite up to coping with life; and this affair about Louisa and Benton and Robby Coles and everybody else had completely unhinged her. Weeping, she regarded it, attempted to deal with it, able to think of how simple it would be if her dear husband were alive.

Louisa rolled on her stomach and gazed out moodily at the great tree in the front yard which stood etched against the moonlit sky like a black paper cutout. She rested her chin on her small hands and sighed unhappily.

Now she had to stay in the house until it was all settled. She didn't mind not going to the shop, she liked that part of it. But not being able to do anything else at all, that she didn't like; being cooped up with her doting, moist-eyed mother. And all because of that stupid story.

Louisa rolled on her back abruptly and squirmed irritably on the sheet. She raised up her feet and kicked off the blankets, her flannel gown sliding up her legs with a sighing of cloth as she kicked.

She didn't pull it back down again but lay there in the darkness, feeling the cool air on her flesh. She closed her eyes and tried to summon up the vision of that ride again.

She couldn't. Her aunt had ruined it, ruined everything. Whenever Louisa thought about it now, her aunt's gaunt, accusing face would materialize in her mind, blotting out the dream. She couldn't envision John Benton anymore without summoning up attendant visions of Robby, of Benton's wife, of her mother, her aunt, of the glittering-eyed Mrs. DeWitt, Mrs. Cartwright and all the women who had come to her aunt's shop to see her and gloat and imagine things.

Louisa felt her cheeks getting warm and she turned quickly and pressed her face into the cool pillowcase. Terrible women! She wasn't going to be like them when *she* grew up.

She felt the air settle like cool silk over her bare calves and thighs as she lay there. It was such an awful thing, gossip. All she'd wanted to do was make Robby a little jealous, get him to do something besides talk in monotones and be boring. Granted, she hadn't chosen her words too wisely but she hadn't meant any harm. And now . . . Louisa blew out a weary breath and felt the heat of it mask her face.

What was going to happen now? she wondered.

Aunt Agatha had spoken about someone paying but, after all, what could Aunt Agatha do? Of course, Robby had gotten very angry and maybe he'd do something. Nothing really dangerous, though. No one would dare try to fight John Benton, that was certain.

Relieved at the acceptance of that, Louisa rolled onto her back again and stared up at the ceiling. Oh, well, so she stayed home a few days. What difference did that make? At least she wouldn't have to work in Aunt Agatha's shop and be stared at by those awful women.

With child. The thought came suddenly and Louisa's throat moved and, for a moment, she could hardly breathe. She knew whose child they meant and she knew how children were begotten.

"*John.*" She whispered it within the shell of dreams she suddenly withdrew to.

Chapter Nineteen

It was nearly midnight. The brass hands of the hall clock hovered a breath apart as Jane Coles closed the door behind herself and moved silently along the hall rug.

At the door to Robby's room, she hesitated a moment, holding the robe closed at her throat. She stared down at her frail fingers curled around the cool metal of the doorknob and there was a slight clicking in her throat as she swallowed.

Then, after a moment, her hand slipped from the knob and fell against her leg and there was a loosening of muscles around her mouth. She turned away.

After a step, she hesitated again, her face tight with nervous indecision. She stood there silently in the cool hall, looking with hopeless eyes at the door to her and Matthew's bedroom, visualizing the immobile bulk of her husband stretched out on the bed, his mouth lax, the firm authority of it gone with the teeth that lay submerged in water on the bedside table, his snores pulsing rhythmically in his throat.

Her lips pressed together suddenly and she turned back. Her fingers closed over the doorknob and, with silent quickness, she entered Robby's bedroom.

The pale moonlight fell across the empty bed.

Jane Coles caught her breath and felt a sudden harsh

sensation in her stomach as if her insides were falling. Then she turned and hurried out of the dark room and down the hall and stairs, a cold hand clamped over her heart.

In the downstairs hall she stopped, then, abruptly, leaned against the wall and listened with a drained weakness to the sound of Robby clearing his throat in the kitchen, the attendant sound of a cup being placed onto its saucer.

After a moment, she drew in a long breath and pushed away from the wall.

As she came through the swinging door, Robby looked up with a nervous jerk of his head, the dark pupils of his eyes expanding suddenly. She saw his Adam's apple move and a nervous smile twitch on his lips.

"Oh . . . it's you, mother," he said.

Jane Coles smiled at the only person in the world she really loved, for some reason, never having been able to feel the devotion toward Jimmy that she did for her older son.

"Can't you sleep, darling?" she asked, walking up to the table where he sat, seeing a thin drift of steam rising from the coffee cup in front of him.

Robby swallowed. "No, I . . ." He didn't finish or pretend he had a finish for the sentence. He lowered his eyes and stared into the cup.

Jane Coles shuddered. She loved Robby so much and yet she could never speak to him nor get him to speak to her. There was always a barrier between them. Maybe, Jane Coles had sometimes thought, it was because Robby needed someone strong to love and encourage him and she was weak, vacillating, without resources. No wonder then he couldn't confide in her and seek out her judgment. No wonder then he could do no more than love her as his mother and avoid looking for anything else in her.

"Are you hungry, son?" she asked.

"No . . . mother, I'm all right."

She stood there, wordless, the smile fixed to her tired face, wanting desperately to speak to him, to have him need her sympathy and love.

Impulsively, she drew out a chair and Robby looked up in poorly veiled surprise as the chair leg grated on the floor. His mother smiled quickly at him and sat down, feeling the pulsebeat throbbing in her wrists. The sickness of despair was coming over her again. Robby was her own son, the only one she really cared for and yet she could not speak of a situation which might lead him to his death.

She swallowed and clasped her hands in her lap until the blood was squeezed from them. She *had* to speak of it.

"Son," she said, her voice a strengthless sound.

Robby looked up at her. "What, mother?"

"You . . ." She looked down quickly at her white hands, then up again. "You've . . . made up your mind?"

"About what, mother?" he asked quietly.

She didn't say anything because she knew he was aware of what she spoke about. She looked at him intently, feeling as if the room and the house had disappeared and there were only the two of them sitting in some immeasurable void together—waiting.

"Yes," he said then and she saw how his fingers twitched restively at the porcelain cup handle. He opened his mouth a little as if he were going to go on, clarifying, explaining. "Yes," he said again.

Mrs. Coles felt as if someone had submerged her in icy, numbing water. She sat there staring at her son, feeling a complete inability in herself, feeling absolutely helpless.

She blinked then, forcing through herself the demand to think, to act.

"Because of Miss Winston's . . . *visit*?"

Robby turned his head away a moment as if he wanted to escape but, after a few seconds, he looked back at her briefly, then at his cup.

"Because of everything," he said.

She stopped the trembling of her lips before she spoke again. "Everything?" she asked.

Robby took a long drink of the coffee and she watched the convulsive movements of his throat muscles. She was about to tell him not to drink coffee or he wouldn't sleep but then she got the sudden idea that if he didn't sleep and was exhausted the next day, his father might not demand anything of him. She remained silent.

Robby clinked down the cup heavily.

"Mother, it's got to be done," he said, his voice tightly controlled. "There's no other way."

The dread again, complete and overwhelming, like a crawling of snakes over her and in her. "But . . . why?" she heard herself asking faintly. "Surely, there's . . ."

Robby twisted his shoulders and she stopped talking, feeling a bolt of anguish at the realization that she was only making it worse for him.

"Mother, there's no other way," he told her in an agitated voice. "If I don't do it, Louisa will never be able to lift her head again in Kellville."

That's his father talking, the thought was like an electric shock in her brain. She stared at him helplessly a moment but then knew suddenly she had to go on because, if she didn't, his decision would remain the same.

"But . . . John Benton didn't admit to doing what . . ." her shoulders twitched nervously, ". . . what they said he did."

"It's not enough, mother," Robby said, almost angrily now. "Can't you see that? The whole town believes he did it and . . ." he punched a fist on his leg, ". . . and Louisa is suffering for it. I have to speak for her, mother, can't you see that I have to?"

She sat in the chair shivering, staring at his tense young face, knowing that he was trying desperately to hang on to his resolve, feeling, in her body, a twisting and knotting of sick terror for him.

"No . . ." she murmured, hardly realizing it herself. In her mind a dozen different questions flung about in a weave of stricken panic. But you didn't ask Louisa if it were true, did you? Why should John Benton do such a thing? Why do you believe everything they tell you? Why do you let them all make your decision for you? Robby, it's your *life*! There's only one! A rushing torrent of words she could never speak to him in a hundred years.

"What are . . . what are you going to do?" she asked, without meaning to.

They were both silent, looking at each other and Jane Coles could hear the clock in the hall ticking away the moments.

Then her son said, "There's only one thing."

Her hand reached out instinctively and closed over his as a rush of horror enveloped her.

"No, darling!" she begged him. "Please don't! *Please!*"

Robby bit his lip and there was a strained sound in his throat as if he had felt himself about to cry and fought it away. He drew his hand from her quickly, his face hardening and, for a hideous moment, Jane Coles saw the face of her husband reflected on Robby's pale features.

"*There's nothing else, I said,*" he told her tensely.

"But not with—!" She broke off suddenly, afraid even of the word.

"Yes," he said and she could see clearly how hard he was trying to believe it himself. "There's no other way a man like him would understand. It's all he deserves. He won't apologize or . . ." He saw the straining fear on her face and his voice snapped angrily. "I believe Louisa! She wouldn't lie to me! Not about something like this. It's my duty to . . . to defend her honor."

"Oh dear God!" Jane Coles slumped over, pressing

her shaking hands to her face. "Dear God, it's your father talking, it's not you. It's him, him! Oh, dear God, dear *God . . .*" The tears ran between her trembling fingers.

Robby sat there stiffly, staring at his mother with half-frightened eyes, desperately afraid that he was going to cry too. He leaned back in the chair looking at her with an expression in his eyes that shifted from resolution to pitying contrition and back to resolute strength again.

"You don't have to cry, mother," he said, feeling a twinge at the cold sound of his voice. "I'm not afraid of John Benton. I . . . I'm not a little boy anymore, mother, I'm twenty-one."

His mother looked up with an anguished sob. "You're not old enough for this!" she cried, almost a fierce anger in her voice. "You mustn't fight him, son, you mustn't!"

She kept crying and, for some strange reason, Robby felt suddenly remorseless and cold toward his sobbing mother. There was no strength in her, the thought crept vaguely through his brain, there was only weakness and surrender. He was a man now and he had a job to do. He was going to do it no matter what happened.

He wished it was morning so he could buckle on his gun and get it over with. He found to his astonishment that he actually *wasn't* afraid of Benton now, that he wanted only to get the job over with. Louisa was his intended bride; someday she would be his wife. His father was right; he had to defend her, now and always, it was his responsibility. When men stopped fighting for their women, the society *would* fail, he was certain of it.

"Go to bed, mother," he said in a flat, emotionless tone, "there's nothing to cry about."

Jane Coles sat slumped on her chair, still weeping, her thin shoulders palsied with sobbing. Robby sat looking at her as he would look at a stranger. He felt cold inside, hollowed out by determination, drained of fear, empty of all but the one resolution he knew he had to obey.

He had said tomorrow. Tomorrow it would be.

Slowly, consciously, his fingers closed on the table top; they made a hard, white fist.

Twelve twenty-one, the end of the second day.

The Third Day

Chapter Twenty

Julia was just putting the rack of loaves into the hot oven when the hound began barking outside the kitchen door at the muffled drumming of hoofbeats. Pushing up the oven door, she moved quickly across the floor toward the window and looked out.

A sudden weakness dragged at her and she caught at the windowsill, her heart suddenly pumping in slow, heavy beats as she saw who it was.

The chestnut gelding was reined up to a careful stop before the house and stood there fidgeting while the hound cringed nearby, ears back, head snapping with each hoarse, excited bark it gave.

"*Benton!*" Julia heard Matthew Coles call out and her stomach muscles shuddered at the sound.

"No," she murmured without realizing it, gasping to draw breath into her lungs.

"Benton!" Coles shouted again, his voice sharp and demanding. Julia stared out at him, hoping desperately that he would think no one was home and ride away.

Then Matthew Coles started to dismount and she pushed from the window and opened the door with a spasmodic pull.

Matthew Coles twitched back, face whitening.

"I am unarm—!" he started to cry out, then broke

off with a tightening of his mouth when he saw it was her.

"Where is your husband, Mrs. Benton?" he asked quickly, trying to cover up his momentary panic. The hound dog backed toward Julia as she stood in the doorway.

"Why do you want to know?" she asked, weakly.

"Mrs. Benton, I expect an answer."

She drew in a shaking breath. "He's not here," she said.

"Where *is* he?"

She swallowed quickly and stared at him, feeling sick and dizzy.

"Mrs. Benton, I demand an—"

"Why do you want to know?"

"That is not your concern, ma'm," said Matthew Coles.

"It's about Louisa Harper, isn't it?" she asked suddenly.

His face hardened. "Where is your husband, ma'm?" he asked.

"Mister Coles, it isn't true! My husband had nothing to do with that girl!"

"I'm afraid the facts speak differently, ma'm," Matthew Coles said with imperious calm. "Now, where is he?"

"Mister Coles, I beg of you—listen to me! My husband had nothing to do with Louisa Harper, I sw—"

"Where is your husband, Mrs. Benton?"

"I swear to you, Mister—"

"Where *is* he, Mrs. Benton?" Matthew Coles asked, his voice rising.

"Why won't you listen to me? Don't you think I'd know?"

"Mrs. Benton, I demand an answer!"

"What are you trying to do—kill your son?!"

The hint of a smile played at Matthew Coles' lips. "I don't believe it's my son you're concerned for," he said.

"Who else would I be concerned for?" she answered heatedly. "You don't think he'd have a chance against my husband, do you? For the love of God, stop this terrible thing before—"

Matthew Coles turned on his heel and lifted his boot toe into the stirrup.

"Mister Coles!" Her cry followed him as she took a quick step into the morning sunlight, face pale and tense.

He said nothing but swung up into the saddle and pulled his horse around.

"You've got to believe me!" she cried. "My husband didn't—"

The rest of her words were drowned out by the quickening thud of the gelding's hooves across the yard.

"*No!*" She screamed it after him.

Then she stood there in the hot blaze of sunlight, shivering uncontrollably, watching him ride away while the hound dog stood beside her, whining.

Suddenly she started running for the barn on trembling legs, breath falling from her lips in gasping bursts. Then, equally as sudden, she stopped, realizing that she didn't know how to hitch up the buckboard for herself. She stood indecisively, halfway between the barn and the house, her chest jerking with frustrated, frightened sobs.

Chapter Twenty-one

"**W**ell, them damn churnheads is in the bog again," was the first thing Joe Bailey said as Benton and Lew Goodwill rode up to him.

"Oh, for—!" Benton hissed angrily. Then he shrugged. "Well . . . stay here with the rest of the herd and Lew and I'll fetch 'em out."

"Okay, boss," Joe Bailey said and Benton and Goodwill rode off toward the mud hole, stopping off at the small range shack for short-handled shovels.

"It's this damn heat," Lew said as the two of them dismounted by the bog. "They try to get cool and all they get is stuck."

Benton grunted and they walked across the rilled ground toward the almost dry spring. As they walked, they saw the two steers struggling in the wire and heard the bellowing of their complaints.

"Sure. Tell us your troubles," Benton said to them under his breath. "If you weren't so damn mule-headed, you wouldn't get *stuck* in there." But he knew it was really because he didn't have enough men to keep a closer watch on the herd. How could one man keep tabs on two hundred head?

As they came to the edge of the mud hole, Benton

and Lew unbuckled their gunbelts and lay them on the top of a boulder.

"Let's get the wrinkle-horn out first," Benton said.

"Right," Lew said and they struggled out into the viscous mud toward the older steer with its wrinkled, scaly horns. Benton gritted his teeth as the smell of hot slime surrounded him.

"Oh, *shut* up!" he snapped as the steer bellowed loudly, trying, in vain, to dislodge its legs.

Quickly, with angrily driven shovel strokes, Benton dug around the steer's legs. The steer kept struggling, sometimes sinking deeper into the hot, reeking muck, its angry, frightened bellows blasting at Benton's eardrums.

Once, its muzzle crashed against Benton's shoulder as he straightened up for a moment and knocked him onto his side, getting his Levi's and shirt mud-coated. Jumping up, he grabbed hold of the scaly horn and shoved the steer's head away with a curse, then started digging again.

Finally, he'd freed most of the front leg and, stepping over the back leg, he started working on that quickly so the mud wouldn't come back around the free leg. On the other side of the struggling steer, he heard his own curses echoed by Lew Goodwill.

"Damn fool!" Lew snapped. "Stop *fussin'* so!"

As he dug, trying to breathe through his clenched teeth, Benton felt great sweat drops trickling down the sides of his chest from his armpits. He kept digging, plunging the shovel point in and hurling the black mud away with angry arm jerks. It's times like this—he thought—when I wish I was back in the Rangers where the only thing a man has to worry about is getting shot.

He hadn't slept much the night before. Julia had kept talking about Robby Coles and he was still thinking about it when he fell into an uneasy doze.

He dreamed that Matthew Coles was tying him to a

hitching post while Robby stood nearby, waiting to fire slugs into him. When the first bullets had struck, he'd jolted up on the bed with a grunt, wide awake.

Then Lew Goodwill had ridden in from the first night watch and said he thought there better be another man to help Joe Bailey on the second watch because there was some electric lightning in the sky and the herd was getting spooky.

Benton had dressed and ridden out to the herd and stayed with Joe a couple of hours until the lightning was gone. Then he'd ridden back to the house. In all, he'd gotten about three hours of sleep.

"All right, get on your horse," he said to Lew.

"Ain't finished the back leg, boss."

"I'll get it, I'll get it," Benton snapped. "Get on your horse."

"Okay." Lew slogged out of the mud hole and moved up to where his horse was tied. He cinched up the saddle as tightly as the latigo straps could be drawn, then led the animal down to the edge of the mud hole.

"All right, toss in your rope," Benton said.

Lew lifted the rope coil off his saddle horn and shook it loose, then tossed one end of it to Benton who tied it securely around the steer's horns. While he did that, Lew fastened the other rope end around his saddle horn and drew it taut. Mounting then, he backed off his sturdy piebald until the lariat was taut.

"All right," Benton called, "drag her out!"

The piebald dug in its hooves and started pulling at the dead weight of the steer. Dust rose under its slipping, straining legs and the muscles of its body stood out like sheathed cables. In the mud hole, Benton shoved at the steer from behind, trying to avoid the spray of mud from its flailing legs but not always succeeding.

"Come on, you wall-eyed mule!" Benton gasped furiously as he shoved the steer, his muscles straining violently.

Slowly, the steer was pulled loose and dragged up

onto hard ground. When they tailed it up, it charged Benton and he had to make a zig-zag dash for the bush. Then Lew chased the steer off and they went back into the mud for the second one.

By the time they had that one out, they were both spattered with mud from head to knee and caked solid below that. They sat in the shade a little while, panting and cursing under their breath.

They were sitting like that when the gelding came over the rise. "Who's that?" Lew asked.

Benton looked up and sudden alarm tightened his face. "My gun," he muttered, and stood up quickly as Matthew Coles spurred his gelding down the gradual slope and reined up.

"What do you want?" Benton asked, realizing that Coles was unarmed.

"I'm here as second for my son," Coles said, stiffly.

"You're what?" Benton squinted up at the older man.

"You will be in town by three o'clock this afternoon to defend yourself," stated Matthew Coles.

Benton stared up incredulously. "What did you say?"

"You heard what I said, sir!"

Benton felt the heat and the dirt and the exhaustion all well up in him and explode as anger. "God damn it, get off my ranch! I told you that girl lied! Now—"

"Either you come in like a man," Matthew Coles flared, "or my son will ride out after you!"

Benton felt like dragging the older man off his horse and pitching him head first into the mud hole. His body shook with repression of the desire.

"Listen," he said. "For the last time, you tell your kid that—"

"By three, Mister Benton. Three o'clock this afternoon."

"Coles, I swear to God, if you don't—"

Matthew Coles pulled his horse around and rode quickly up the incline as Benton started forward, his face suddenly whitening with fury.

Benton stopped and watched the older man ride away.

"He's loco," Lew Goodwill said then and Benton glanced over at the big man. "He's tryin' to kill his own kid," Lew went on. "He *must* be loco."

Benton walked away on stiff legs and stood by the boulder buckling on his gunbelt. What was he supposed to do now, he wondered. Did he stay out on the ranch and wait to see if Robby Coles really would come after him? It was what he felt like doing. Without any trouble at all, he could convince himself that the kid wasn't going to commit suicide.

But he didn't try to convince himself. He stood there worriedly, staring at the crest of the slope where Matthew Coles had disappeared.

Finally, he exhaled a heavy breath and groaned because he knew what he had to do. "Oh . . . *damn!*" he muttered to himself and started in quick, angry strides for his horse.

"I'll be back as soon as I can," he told Lew. "Tell Merv and Joe I . . ." Another disgusted hiss of breath. "Tell 'em I have to go into the damn town again."

"Take it easy, boss," Lew said and Benton grunted a reply as he started up the slope.

As he swung into the saddle, he ran his right hand across his brow and slung away the sweat drops on his fingers. Then he nudged his spurs into the horse's flanks and felt the animal charge up the incline beneath him.

What do I do first? The thought plagued him as he galloped for the ranch. Should he try Robby first or his father, Louisa or her aunt or her mother, the Reverend Bond or maybe even the sheriff? He didn't know. All he knew was that things were too damn complicated. Some stupid little girl makes up a story about him and, in two days, everybody expects him to defend his life.

It was hard not to let them have their way. Certainly he was fed up enough just to let it happen the way they wanted. But then he knew again that killing Robby wasn't the answer. Robby wasn't any villain to be killed; he was only a pawn.

Why did I leave the Rangers? He was asking himself the question again as he rode up to the house and jumped off his horse.

Julia was in the doorway before he'd even tied up the panting mount.

"John," she said breathlessly, staring at his mud-spattered clothes.

"It's all right," he said quickly as she ran to him.

"*Oh.*" She swallowed and caught his hand. "Mud. I thought—" She swallowed again and didn't finish. "What happened, John?" she asked instead.

He told her briefly as he went into the house, pulling off his mud-caked shirt and starting to wash up at the pump.

"What are you going to do?" she asked, apprehensively.

"Go into town," he said. "No, I'm not takin' a gun with me," he added quickly, seeing the look in her eyes. "I'll try talkin' reason to them again." He dashed water in his face and washed off the soap. "There must be *one* of them that'll listen to reason. I sure can't see shootin' that kid over nothin' at all."

"I want to go with you," Julia said, suddenly.

"No, I'll get there faster by myself," he told her.

"John, I want to go," she said again and this time it wasn't just a request. He looked over at her as he lathered his muddy arms.

"Honey, who's goin' to feed the boys? They gotta have their chuck, you know."

"They can manage by themselves one day," she said. "I'll leave the food on the table."

"Julia, there isn't that much time."

"Then I'll leave a note telling them where everything is," she argued. "If there isn't much time, it's even more important that I go with you. There may be a lot of people to see and two of us can do more than one.

And—besides—the women are more likely to listen to me than you." She spoke quickly, submerging the rise of dread in a tide of rapid planning.

Benton hesitated a moment longer, looking at her intent face. Then he turned away with a shrug. "All right," he said, wearily. As she sat down to write the note, she heard him muttering to himself about how the ranch was going to go to hell because of all this lost time.

"We'll tie Socks behind the buckboard," she said, looking up from the note, "then, when we get into town, we can separate and get more done that way."

"Well, there isn't much time," Benton said, looking at the clock, "it's almost eleven now. It'll take till quarter of twelve to reach town even if we push it."

"He didn't set a time, did he?" she asked, her voice suddenly faint.

"Three," he said.

"This afternoon?" She knew even as she said it that it had to be that afternoon. "Oh, dear God."

Benton grunted, then turned from the pump. "I'm goin' to change clothes now," he said. "Will you get Socks and the dark mare outta the barn? I'll put the other one away before we leave."

He headed for the bedroom.

"John," she said suddenly when he was almost out of the kitchen. He looked back over his shoulder.

"John . . . promise me that . . ." she swallowed, ". . . that whatever happens you won't . . ." She couldn't finish.

They looked at each other a long moment and it seemed as if the great conflict in their life and marriage were a wall being erected between them again.

Then John said, "There's no time to talk now," and left her staring at the place where he'd been standing. She listened to the sound of her pencil hitting the floor and rolling across the boards.

Chapter Twenty-two

The two women sat in the front room. They both had yarn and needles in their laps but only one of them was knitting; that was Agatha Winston. Her sister sat without moving, her limpid eyes unfocused, on her face a look of disconcerted reflection.

Miss Winston looked up. "You'll never finish the shawl like that," she said, curtly.

Elizabeth Harper's hands twitched in her lap and her gaze lifted for a moment to the carved features of her sister.

"I can't," she said then, with an unhappy sigh.

Agatha Winston's thin lips pressed a grimace into her face and she went back to her knitting without another word.

In the hall, the clock chimed a hollow stroke and then eleven more. Elizabeth Harper sat listening, her hands clasped tightly in her lap, her eyes on the calmly moving fingers of Agatha Winston. Noon, she thought, it's noon.

"How can you be so—?" she began to say and then was halted by the coldness in her sister's eyes.

Miss Winston put down her work. "What is happening," she said, "is beyond our control. It had to be this way. John Benton made it so." She picked up her work again. "And there's no point in our dwelling on it," she said.

Elizabeth Harper stirred restlessly on the chair. "But that poor boy," she murmured. "What will happen to him?"

"He is not a boy, Elizabeth."

"But he's not . . ." Mrs. Harper looked upset. "Oh . . . how can he hope to do anything against that . . . that awful man?"

Miss Winston breathed in deeply. "It is what he has to do," was all she said. "Let's not talk about it."

Elizabeth Harper looked back at her hands, feeling her body tighten as she thought about Robby Coles going against a man who had lived by violence for—how many years? She bit her lip. It was terrible, it was a terrible thing. If only her dear husband were alive; he'd have found a way to avoid violence. Indeed, he'd have raised Louisa so strictly that this terrible thing would never have happened in the first place. She'd been unable to control the girl since Mr. Harper died. Oh, why was he dead, why?

She brushed away an unexpected tear, looking up guiltily to see if Agatha had seen; but Miss Winston was absorbed in knitting.

Three o'clock, Mrs. Harper thought. Less than three hours now. It was terrible, terrible.

"You're . . . certain he said—?" she started.

"What?" Agatha Winston looked up irritably.

Elizabeth Harper swallowed. "You're . . . sure he said three o'clock?"

"That is what he said," Miss Winston answered, looking back to her work. She'd met Matthew Coles that morning on the way to her shop and he'd told her that Robby was going to meet John Benton in the square at three o'clock that afternoon. After she'd heard that, she'd gone immediately to her sister's house to see personally that Louisa remained in the house all day. Naturally, she'd have to leave the shop closed all day too.

"What is it?" she asked, pettishly, hearing Elizabeth speak her name again.

Mrs. Harper swallowed nervously. "Don't you . . . think we should tell Louisa?"

"Of course I don't think we should tell her," Miss Winston said sharply. "Hasn't she enough to be concerned with without worrying more?"

"But . . . what if Robby . . . ?" Mrs. Harper dared not finish the sentence.

Miss Winston spoke clearly and authoritatively.

"We will not think about it," she declared.

Upstairs, Louisa was standing restively by the window, looking out at the great tree in the front yard. She'd come up to her room shortly after breakfast when her Aunt Agatha had arrived at the house. Since then, a strange uneasiness had oppressed her.

What was Aunt Agatha doing at their house? She hadn't missed opening her shop one day in the past twelve years—outside of Sundays, of course. No one was more strict in her habits than Aunt Agatha. No shop owner could have been more religious in his hours. At nine, the shop was unlocked, dusted, and prepared for the day's business. At twelve it was shut for dinner, at one, reopened, and, promptly at five, it was locked up for the night. Now, *this*—Aunt Agatha sitting down in the front room with her mother. They'd been there almost three hours now . . .

. . . as if they were waiting for something.

Louisa bit her lower lip and her breasts trembled with a harsh breath. Something was wrong, she could feel it. But what could be wrong? Certainly Robby wasn't going to . . . no, that was ridiculous, he knew better than that. Maybe something was happening but not that, it couldn't be that. Maybe Robby and his father were going out to ask John Benton about the story she'd told. That was bad enough—the idea made her sick with dread of what would happen if Aunt Agatha found out she'd lied.

But that was all, that was the worst that could happen.

Then why was Aunt Agatha downstairs with her mother? Why hadn't Aunt Agatha spoken more than a few words to her that morning, suggesting, almost as soon as she was in the house, that Louisa go up to her room?

Louisa turned from the window and walked in quick, nervous steps across the floor, her small hands closed into fists swinging at her sides. For some reason, her throat felt constricted and she had trouble breathing. For some reason, the muscles in her stomach felt tight as if she were about to be sick—even though there was no reason for it.

She sank down on the bed and forced herself to pick up her embroidery. Then, in a few moments, she put it down on the bedside table again and stroked restless fingers at the skirt of her gingham dress.

No, there was something wrong. No matter how she tried to explain things to herself, she couldn't find any good reason for Aunt Agatha to be there. Not if everything was all right, not if the story she'd told was being forgotten. No, there was something—

Louisa started as she heard the sound of hooves out front, the rattling squeak of a buckboard. Quickly, heart beating, she jumped up and hurried to the window.

Her breath caught as she saw John Benton's wife climbing down off the buckboard in front of the house and, unconsciously, a look of apprehensive dread contorted her face. With frightened eyes, she watched Mrs. Benton open the gate and shut it behind her.

Suddenly, she jerked back as Mrs. Benton glanced up at the window. She pressed herself against the wall, feeling her chest throb with great, frantic heartbeats. Why was Mrs. Benton here? Louisa fought down a sob and dug her teeth into her lip. Fear welled over her like rising waters. Mrs. Benton was going to tell Aunt Agatha the truth and then Aunt Agatha would know everything. She brushed away the sudden tears spilling from her eyes.

Then she stiffened against the wall as the front doorbell tinkled. She stood there, petrified, listening.

Downstairs, there were footsteps.

Suddenly, Louisa found herself pressing off her shoes and rushing across the room to open the door, then moving stealthily into the hall. As she edged cautiously for the head of the stairs, she heard the footsteps halting at the front door.

"*Oh!*" She heard her mother gasp and then the footsteps again and the almost inaudible sound of her mother and aunt talking guardedly. Louisa crouched down by the bannisters and listened, her chest twitching with panic-stricken heartbeats.

Footsteps again—her aunt's; she knew they were Aunt Agatha's, there was something about the way Aunt Agatha walked. Louisa's hands froze on the bannister she was clutching and there was a clicking in her throat.

Downstairs, she heard Aunt Agatha clear her throat. Then the doorknob was turned and her aunt was saying, "Yes?" in that cold, unreceptive way she had.

"*Oh.*" Mrs. Benton sounded surprised. Then she said, "Miss Winston, I'd like to talk to your sister."

"Oh?" Aunt Agatha's voice was still chilled and unwelcoming.

There was a moment's pause, then the hesitant voice of Mrs. Benton saying, "May . . . I come in?"

Aunt Agatha drew in a quick breath. "I'm afraid not," she said and Louisa felt a cold shudder run down her back. "My niece is indisposed," Agatha Winston added and Louisa felt the skin tightening on her face.

"Miss Winston, please. I don't believe you realize what's happening."

Her aunt's voice hard and controlled, saying, "I know exactly what is happening." Louisa didn't realize that she was holding her breath as she pressed her paling cheek against the hard bannister. *What's happening?* The words dug at her.

"Well, then, you must know how serious it is," Mrs. Benton said, "This terrible thing has to be stopped before it's too late."

"It *is* too late, Mrs. Benton," Agatha Winston's voice said.

"But it isn't," Julia Benton said quickly. "It can still be avoided."

Another pause. Louisa drew in a quick, wavering breath, listening intently.

"Miss Winston, you simply must—"

"Mrs. Benton," Agatha Winston interrupted, "I'm afraid there's nothing I can do to help you. The situation is quite out of my hands. I . . . don't like to say it but—well, your husband should have considered the consequences before he—"

"But that's the whole point, Miss Winston!" Julia Benton exclaimed, "He didn't do it! He's had nothing to do with your niece—*nothing*!"

Louisa's eyes closed suddenly and she felt herself shivering helplessly. Now everyone would know, now she'd be punished. Oh God, I want to die! she thought in an agony of shame—I want to *die*!

"I would like to believe that," her aunt said to Mrs. Benton then, "but I'm afraid it's gone too far for that."

"Too far?" Julia Benton sounded stunned. "How can it have gone so far you won't listen to the truth?"

Louisa felt numbed as she pressed against the bannister, her fingers clutching whitely at it. She heard her aunt say, a little less assuredly now, "I told you, Mrs. Benton, the matter is out of my hands."

"It's not out of Louisa's hands!"

Louisa gasped. Now, she thought in terror, *now* Aunt Agatha would find out and everyone would know . . .

But her aunt said, "It is out of her hands too," an undertone of anger in her voice.

"Dear God, what's the matter with everybody!" Julia Benton burst out. "Do you all want Robby killed!"

Up on the landing, Louisa couldn't breathe suddenly. She felt as if her heart had stopped, her blood had ceased to flow, as if every function of her body had stopped in that instant. On her drained face, a look of utter horror froze.

Robby *killed*?

She hardly heard her aunt speak out angrily, "How dare you accuse us of that!"

"What else can I say when you won't listen to facts!"

"I think you'd better go, Mrs. Benton."

"I must see Louisa."

"I've already told you—!"

"I know what you told me! But I'm not going to stand by and watch that boy killed over nothing!"

Louisa flinched at the word, her lips trembling and cold. I didn't know, I didn't know—the words stumbled in her shocked mind—oh God, I didn't *know*.

Now, downstairs, her aunt suddenly cried out, "You're not coming in here!"

"Miss Winston, you don't know what you're doing!"

"I am in full sympathy with your concern, Mrs. Benton," Miss Winston said, her words tightly articulated, "but I cannot allow you to upset my niece any further. If you want to argue with anyone, argue with Mister Coles and his son. The matter is—"

"Miss Winston, there isn't time!"

"—in their hands now, not ours!" Miss Winston finished her sentence loudly.

"Miss Winston, Louisa is the only one who can—"

The loud slamming of the front door cut off Julia Benton's frantic voice and made Louisa start violently, her hands tightening spasmodically on the bannister. Downstairs, she heard a drawn-in breath rasp in her aunt's throat, then a choked sob. The doorbell rang insistently.

"Go away!" Agatha Winston cried out in a broken voice. "You're not welcome here!"

Suddenly, Louisa pushed herself up and moved around the bannister railing, desperately thinking— I've got to stop it!

The sight of her aunt drove her back and a whimper started in her throat as she drew away from the head of the stairs. No, no, I have to tell her!—she thought in terrified anguish.

She whirled and ran down the hall, her feet soundless on the thick rug. Pushing open the door, she shut it quickly and silently behind herself and rushed across the room toward the window.

As she reached it, she saw Julia Benton moving for the gate. Her mouth opened and she tried to call to her but the sound would not come—it froze in her throat. In her mind a flood of frightened thoughts drowned resolve—Aunt Agatha finding out, Robby finding out, John Benton finding out, the whole town finding out . . .

A sob broke in her throat and her hands clutched desperately at the windowsill. But I have to tell! she thought, agonized, I can't let him be *killed*!

"Mrs. Benton!" she called. But the call was a strangled whispering and, with sickened eyes, she watched Julia Benton get in the buckboard.

Then Mrs. Benton looked at the house, her face white and shaken. Louisa raised her hand suddenly. "Mrs. *Benton*!" she said, a little louder but not loud enough.

Julia Benton tugged at the dark reins and the horse pulled the buckboard away.

"No!" Louisa couldn't keep from crying out. She clapped a shaking hand over her mouth and whirled to face the door. Had Aunt Agatha heard her? She stared at the closed door for a full minute, lips shaking, her eyes stark with dread.

Aunt Agatha did not come up. Louisa leaned back against the wall weakly, her mind confused with a tangling of thoughts. What was she going to do? Oh God, what was she going to *do*?

Out in the hall, a wall clock ticked its endless beat while the minute hand moved slowly for the number six. In ten minutes, it would be twelve-thirty.

Chapter Twenty-three

"**H**e's out of town," Benton told her when they met at the foot of Davis Street.

Julia stared up at him blankly. "Out of town?" she repeated in a faint voice.

"That's what the deputy said."

"But . . . for how long?"

"Three days yet," John said gravely. "He's takin' a prisoner to the Rangers." On the plank sidewalk, passing men and women glanced at them and tried to hear what they were saying.

"Well, what about the deputy?" Julia said. "He can stop it, can't he?"

"Well—" John started to say, then glanced over suddenly at the sidewalk where two men looked away and walked off quickly along the planks toward the Zorilla Saloon.

Mouth tightened, Benton dismounted and tied Socks to the back of the buckboard. A thin-wheeled rig came crackling up Davis Street and was guided around them. From the corners of his eyes, Benton saw Henry Oliver looking at him curiously.

Then the rig turned left into the square and Benton climbed up on the seat beside Julia.

"He won't do anything," he told her. "Too many

people are for it. Guess this thing is bigger than we thought. Half the town knows about it, looks like."

"But . . ." Julia stared at him, dazedly, trying to think but unable to, ". . . what are we going to do?"

John didn't even bother shrugging. "I don't know, ma," he said quietly, looking at his hands. "I just don't know." He looked up at her. "What happened at the girl's house?"

"Her aunt was there," Julia said.

"She wouldn't even let you *in*, I expect," John said grimly and she started to say something but didn't. They sat there in the motionless buckboard, trying to ignore the passersby who stared at them.

"Well, let's not just *sit* here," John said abruptly. "Here, you want me to drive?" He reached for the reins, then glanced up irritably at a passing man who was gaping at him.

"Give me the reins, Julia," he said tersely.

She looked over at him. "Where are we going?" she asked, worriedly.

His mouth opened a little as if he were about to speak, then he hesitated and blew out a tired breath.

"Where *can* we go?" he asked her.

"Well . . ."

"We'll have to go back to the ranch," he said.

"John, we can't."

"Julia, what else is there to do?"

"Can't we see the deputy sheriff again? He has to keep the peace; it's his job."

"Honey, the job's no bigger than the man. Catwell's just a store clerk with a badge on. He's not goin' to stand up against half the town. He's not the kind."

"But we *can't* go back, John," she said, more heatedly. "We've got to stop it somehow."

"What would you suggest?" he asked, his voice flat and unencouraging.

"I don't know," she said, trying to get control of her scattered thoughts. "But we have to do something."

John shrugged and let his hands fall to his lap and he sat there staring at his mud-caked boots.

"I almost think you want this—" Julia started to say, then stopped as he looked over quickly at her. "I'm sorry, I'm sorry, John," she said hastily. "It's just that . . ."

She pressed her hands together. "Can't we . . ." She hesitated and then said quickly, "We'll go talk to Robby."

"Honey, you heard his old man this morning," John said. "Did he sound like he was open to reason?"

"We'll talk to Robby, not his father."

"Same thing," he said, disgustedly.

"John, we have to do *some*thing," she said slowly and tensely. "You know we have to."

He let go of the reins and pressed his lips together.

"All right," he said curtly. "All right, Julia. But not much more. You understand? *Not much more.*"

With a nervous twitching of her hands, Julia shook the reins and the buckboard lurched forward into the square.

Chapter Twenty-four

Louisa stood at the head of the stairs, looking down, one hand pressed at the bosom of her dress, the other clamped tightly on the bannister railing.

They were still down there. They weren't talking but Louisa knew they were there and knew she'd have to walk by the front room to get to the kitchen and the back door.

She lowered one foot nervously and shifted her weight to the first carpeted step with a cautious movement. The stair creaked a little and Julia stiffened, her eyes fastened to the doorway below that led to the front room.

There was no sound. Julia brought the other foot down and stood on the top step, legs cold and trembling. Suddenly, she became conscious of the ticking clock and she glanced over at it, her throat moving.

Twenty minutes to one. There was so little time.

She moved down another step silently. I should tell Aunt Agatha, the thought oppressed her, Aunt Agatha could stop it.

But the idea of telling her aunt made Louisa's stomach turn. She couldn't do it, she just couldn't, she'd rather tell anyone else.

Besides, she rationalized weakly, Aunt Agatha had

said it was out of her hands. No, she'd have to tell someone else.

But who?

Louisa moved down another step, her lips twitching as the wood crackled in strain beneath her. I should have taken my shoes off! the thought burst in her mind. What if they heard her? What if they came out in the hall and saw her on the stairs? What would she tell Aunt Agatha; what *could* she tell her?

Louisa stood fixed to the step, heart thudding in heavy, irregular beats. She bit her trembling lip. No, I have to do it! she told herself, fighting off the instinct to rush back to her room and hide. I have to, I just *have* to!

She swallowed the obstruction in her throat and moved down another step, her hand sliding noiselessly along the bannister railing, then clamping tightly as she lowered herself. Another step; another.

She froze involuntarily. Down in the front room, her aunt was clearing her throat.

"Are we having dinner?" she heard Aunt Agatha say.

"If you . . . want some," the pale voice of her mother replied. "I'm . . . not hungry, myself."

"*I am*," said Aunt Agatha.

Louisa shuddered and stood there rooted, expecting at any moment to see her aunt come walking out of the front room.

But there was only silence below. Louisa thought she heard the clicking of knitting needles but she wasn't sure. I have to get out! she thought desperately.

She moved down another step, lowering her foot cautiously, testing her weight on the carpeted wood. Another step. She stopped and tightened as a horse galloped by in front of the house and she thought it was going to stop. She closed her eyes a moment and drew in a heavy, nervous breath. Why wasn't there a back stairway?

"The nerve of that woman," she heard Aunt Agatha say.

"She's just—" her mother started and then said no more.

"Defending him like that," said Agatha Winston in an insulted voice. "The very idea; after what he did."

No, no, I mustn't cry, I mustn't—Louisa begged herself, reaching up hastily to brush aside the tears. Why did she ever tell Robby that story—*why*? She drew in a rasping breath and then cut it off sharply, her eyes widening in fright.

No sound in the front room. She moved down another step and it creaked beneath her.

"Louisa?"

She felt a bolt of panic stun her heart as her aunt's voice probed up at her. She stood there mutely, shivering without control as her aunt came out of the front room, carrying her knitting.

"What is it you want?" her aunt asked.

"I . . ." Louisa stared down dumbly at her.

"Well?"

Louisa tried to speak but there was no sound.

"Speak up, child!"

"I'm hungry." Louisa heard herself blurt out the words.

Her aunt looked up at her suspiciously a moment, then said grumpily, "Oh."

Turning, Aunt Agatha went back into the front room. Now! Louisa thought frantically and she ran down the steps on trembling legs.

"You can't be *that* hungry," Agatha Winston said, coming back into the hall, this time without her knitting.

Louisa felt a sudden cold sinking in her stomach and her legs were numb under her as she walked toward the kitchen, Aunt Agatha following behind her, saying, "Elizabeth? Come along, it's dinner time," and her mother answering, weakly, "Yes . . . Agatha."

Chapter Twenty-five

Julia drew back on the reins and the mare stopped in front of the shop. She pulled back on the brake and stood up. John helped her down without a word, his face hard and thin-lipped. She didn't speak to him as they walked, side by side, across the dirt, then stepped up onto the roofed-over plank sidewalk. John's hand released hers and he opened the door of the shop for her.

The bell over the door tinkled and Matthew Coles looked up from his bench, his face tightening as he saw who it was. Slowly, with carefully controlled movement, he rose and came walking to the front counter. He said nothing, he didn't even look at Benton.

"Mister Coles," Julia said.

"Well?" His voice was hard and unpleasant.

"Mister Coles, this thing has gone far enough," Julia said, trying to sound calm. "It must be stopped—*now.*"

The expression on Matthew Coles' face did not change at all. "Stopped?" he asked as if he were actually curious.

Julia Benton swallowed and Benton pressed his lips together over clenched teeth.

"Mister Coles, my husband is not guilty of what he's been accused. I'll say it again, Mister Coles. He is not guilty. Louisa Harper *lied.*"

Only the slight tensing of skin over his cheekbones betrayed what Matthew Coles felt. His tone remained the same.

"I'm sorry," he said. "We do not believe that."

Julia Benton stared at him, speechless. It's true, she thought, realizing it then in sudden shock, dear God, it was true! They didn't *want* to believe; no one did.

"Of course," Matthew Coles said sonorously, "If your husband wishes to make a public apology and then vacate his ranch, that is something else again."

"Listen, Coles," Benton's deep voice broke in suddenly. Matthew Coles looked over at him, his expression just sly enough, his head just tilted enough to give him a look of arrogant aplomb.

"Yes, Mister Benton," he said.

Benton felt an old, almost forgotten beat churning up in his stomach, an almost forgotten tightening of his right arm muscles.

"I'm givin' it to you straight, Coles," he said tensely, leaning forward slightly. "If you don't stop your kid, he's goin' to get blown apart." Julia gasped but Benton kept on. "You hear me, Coles—I said *blown apart*," he went on. "I'm not foolin', so listen to me."

"I'm listening," Matthew Coles said.

"This whole damn thing is a mistake," Benton said, slowly and distinctly. "Beginning to end it's a mistake. I don't know Louisa Harper, I never spoke a word to her in my life. That's *it*, Coles and that's all I'm sayin'— and all I'm takin'. Don't push your kid into this, Coles. Don't do it. You'll be sorry."

Matthew Coles tried to swallow without showing it.

"Is that all?" he said.

"That's all," Benton said.

"Mister Coles," Julia said, her voice pleading, "I beg of you . . ."

Benton said, "Come on, Julia," his voice low and curt. Her eyes moved frantically to her husband, then back to Matthew Coles again, her lips moving slightly as though she were going to say something.

"I said come *on*, Julia," Benton said, voice a little louder now.

"John, we—"

His strong fingers closed over her arm. "Julia," he said and the way he said it, it was a command.

"Three o'clock, Mister Benton," Matthew Coles said.

Benton's head jerked around and he looked back at Coles, the edge of his jaw whitening in sudden fury.

"That's enough, Coles," he warned.

"If you are not in the square by then," Matthew Coles said, "my son will come out to your ranch and shoot you down like a dog."

Benton turned a little and his cold voice probed into Matthew Coles' ears. "You're mighty free with your son's life, Coles," he said. "I wonder if you'd be as free with your own."

Matthew Coles shuddered but immediately regained his composure. "Get out, Mister Benton," he ordered. "And be thankful at this moment that you have no gun on you . . ."

Benton almost started back after him. Then, with a twitch of muscles, he turned away. "Just remember, it's on your conscience," he said.

Benton led Julia from the shop, his hand tight on her arm. "John," she kept saying. "John. John . . ."

"That's enough, Julia," he said.

"But John, we—"

"I said that's enough," he ordered, helping her up onto the buckboard. He walked around it and climbed onto the other side.

"Do you *want* this fight?" she whispered passionately as he shoved forward the brake and snapped the reins over the mare's back.

"Sure!" he snapped at her. "Sure, that's it! That's all I've been doin' the last two days—lookin' for a fight!"

"John, I didn't mean—"

"Then, watch what you say, for God's sake!"

"John, *please.* Couldn't we go see Robby? He'd be alone at home and—"

"No," he said.

She twisted her shoulders worriedly and bit her lower lip. "Let's go see the Reverend Bond then," she said. "He might—"

"No, Julia, *no,*" he said sternly. "I'm through scraping. I've had enough; I've had *more* than enough."

She sat shivering beside him, staring at his hard-set features as the buckboard rocked and rattled across the square headed for St. Virgil Street, for the edge of town.

In the church steeple, the rust-throated bell tolled and it was one o'clock.

Chapter Twenty-six

"**T**he butter, if you please," said Agatha Winston and, without a word, her sister passed the plate across the table. "Thank you," Agatha Winston said, in a tone that held no gratitude. She sliced herself another piece of bread and spread a paper-thin coating of butter on its porous surface. This she cut into four equal parts with two deft strokes of her knife.

Chewing, she eyed her sister, then her niece, neither of whom were eating.

"I thought you were hungry," she said to Louisa.

Her niece looked up a moment and Agatha Winston saw the nervous swallowing in her throat.

"I . . . guess I'm not," Louisa said.

"You'd better eat *some*thing or you'll get sick," said her aunt. She sliced off a thick piece of bread and dropped it on Louisa's plate. "Put cheese on it," she said. "It's good for you."

"I'm really not . . . not hungry, Aunt Agatha."

"Eat it," said her aunt and, after a moment, Louisa picked up her knife obediently.

"Why are you shaking so?" her aunt asked and Louisa started in her chair.

"I'm . . . cold," she said, lowering her eyes. She felt the probing gaze of her aunt on her as she buttered the bread with nervous movements. She thought she knew what her aunt was thinking—*cold; shaking; that* time of the month; something not spoken of; preferably, not even thought of.

At any other time, knowing or thinking that Aunt Agatha was thinking that would have flushed Louisa's cheek with shamed embarrassment but today it didn't seem important. There was a clock ticking away the time in the hall and there was only one thing important—to get out of the house and find someone who could stop the fight. It was strange but there was no question in her mind about telling her aunt even when she believed that it would end the fight. She had to tell someone else.

After a few token bites, she put down the bread.

"May I be excused?" she asked, wondering what time it was.

"You haven't eaten a thing," said her aunt.

"Perhaps she's . . . not well," Louisa's mother suggested timidly.

"She won't be well if she doesn't eat something."

Outside, in the hall, the pendulum was swinging; one fifteen.

"I *don't* feel well," Louisa followed her mother's lead. "May I be excused?" A plan was suddenly forming in her mind; the two of them at the kitchen table, the front door unguarded.

"You'd better go to your room," said Aunt Agatha.

"Can't I go for a—" Louisa cut off her impulsive words with a shudder.

"For what?" Aunt Agatha challenged.

"N-nothing, Aunt Agath—"

"I hope you have no plans for leaving the house, young miss," Agatha Winston said suspiciously. "You know very well you can't go out and you know why."

Louisa swallowed, feeling the pulsebeat throbbing in her wrists. She shouldn't have mentioned going out.

"All r-ight," she faltered. "I'll go up to my room."

She pushed back her chair and stood, trying to keep

her face composed, trying not to think of the consequences of running from the house against her aunt's orders. "Excuse me," she murmured, her hands cold and trembling as she moved around the table and started for the door.

"I think you'd better lie down for a while," Aunt Agatha told her.

"Yes, Aunt Agatha, I will," she said, then shuddered as she realized she was lying. I don't *care*—she told herself as she pushed through the swinging door and moved along the hall rug toward the door—it doesn't matter anymore what she thinks.

"Where do you think you're going?"

At the sound of her aunt's demanding voice, Louisa's hand jerked off the door handle and twitched down to her side.

She stood there, white-faced, as her aunt stalked up to her.

"Where were you going, Louisa?"

"N-no place."

"Don't lie to me, Louisa!"

In the kitchen doorway, Louisa noticed her mother appear, her face confused and helpless.

"I was just g-going out on the porch," she told her aunt

"Why?"

"I . . . just wanted some air; it's so s-stuffy in my room."

Agatha Winston looked at her doubtfully, her thin lips pinched together.

"I hope you're telling me the truth, Louisa," she said. "I hope so."

"I am, I am."

Agatha Winston gestured toward the staircase. "Go up to your room," she said tersely. "We'll discuss this later."

"Yes, Aunt Ag—"

"*Agatha*," Mrs. Harper said then and Agatha Winston turned. For a moment, the two women looked out at each other and a questioning expression flickered across Elizabeth Harper's face. Agatha seemed to guess what her sister was thinking for she turned back to Louisa quickly.

"Your room," she said.

When Louisa had reached the top of the staircase, Agatha Winston moved to where her sister stood.

"What's the matter with you?" she challenged. "Do you want her to know? Isn't there enough to worry about already?"

"But it doesn't seem fair to—"

"Fair!" Agatha Winston burst out angrily. "Would it be fair to make her sick with worry? Would it?"

Elizabeth Harper looked at her sister and was lost in hopeless confusion. "I don't know," she murmured. "Perhaps . . . you're right. I . . . don't know. If only my dear—"

"I *do* know," snapped Agatha Winston and went back to the stairs to listen for the closing of the upstairs door.

Up in the hallway, Louisa stood leaning against the wall watching the clock pendulum move endlessly from side to side. And there seemed to be a pendulum in her chest too that swung and struck against her heart and her ribs. Back and forth hitting her heart—her ribs—heart—ribs—heart—time passing inexorably.

Her hands shook and there was a great sick churning in her stomach.

Suddenly she sobbed. "*Robby!*" His name fell like a shattered thing from her lips.

In an hour and a half . . .

Chapter Twenty-seven

She'd been silent all the way back to the ranch; silent as he unhitched the mare but left his own horse saddled and tied up in front of the house. Silent as they went into the house and found the kitchen table covered with the remains of the dinner the boys had made for themselves; silent as John went into the bedroom, silent as she stood in the middle of the small kitchen, listening to the sound of his footsteps, the sound of the clock ticking, her eyes fastened to the doorway he would return through. All this time, silent.

But when he came back in, buckling on his gunbelt, she felt herself twitch suddenly and words came.

"John, you can't," she said, "you just can't."

He stopped walking and looked at her, his face strained with unvoiced tensions. For a moment his hands were motionless on the belt buckle. Then they finished up and dropped to his sides and a heavy breath of air expanded his chest before slowly emptying from it.

"I have to," was all he said.

"But why?"

His lips pressed together a little as he stood there looking at her. Then he turned and glanced at the clock. It was almost two.

"I think you know why," he said.

He went over to the stove and opened one of the covers. Dropping in some kindling and crumpled news-paper, he lit them with a sulfur match. Julia stood there, without a word, staring at the pistol butt bobbing slightly on his left hip as he stirred up the flames and put the coffee pot over them.

Suddenly she moved to him and her hands clutched at his arms.

"Just don't go," she said impulsively. "Just refuse to fight him."

He tried to look patient with her but it didn't work. He shook his head once, very slowly.

"But *why*?" she asked again, a tremor in her voice.

"Julia, you know why. You heard what Matt Coles said. If I don't come into town, Robby'll come out here." His head shook again. "I won't have that, Julia," he said.

"But he won't come out."

"You know different," he said calmly. "You know what's behind him, pushin'."

"But he wouldn't shoot you down in cold blood!"

"He would if his father *made* him," John said, a little more loudly now. "No, it's no good, Julia, it's just no good. I'm not goin' to set here and wait for Robby to come out lookin' for me."

"But John, he wouldn't shoot you, he's not that way."

Benton blew out a tired breath and turned back to the stove to move the coffee pot restlessly over the fire.

"Whether he shot me or not," he said, "it'd be the same. I'd be a laughin'stock."

"Laughingstock?" she said, uncomprehendingly. "I don't—"

"I could never ride into town again without bein' laughed at."

"Well who cares about that?" Julia argued. "Isn't it more important that—"

"I care," Benton said, turning abruptly, his face hard

and determined. "I didn't start this fight, Julia; you know I didn't start it. But I'm not lettin' anybody push me into a corner and make a fool of—"

"You'd rather kill, is that it?" she said sharply.

"If that's what you think . . ." Benton didn't finish up but turned slowly to the stove again.

Julia felt herself trembling with nervous anger.

"We'll move then," she said desperately. "We'll go away."

"*What?*" He looked at her incredulously. "After all the work we've put into this place? Just move? What kind of an idea is that?"

"I just don't want you to fight that boy!" she flared up at him.

His face stiffened as if he were about to yell back at her but he repressed it instantly.

"Listen, Julia," he said, "I've done everything you ever asked of me. I finally left the Rangers because you couldn't take worryin' anymore, it wasn't just the Grahams. I never wore a gun in the town, I only wore it on the ranch. I didn't even join that posse though I should have. But don't ask me to back out of this."

"You said you'd never put on a gun against anyone as long as you lived," she said in a hollow voice.

He looked at her as if he couldn't believe what he'd heard.

"Julia, what do you want me to do—forget I'm a man? Creep away from this fight? *I* didn't start the damn thing, I didn't have a thing to do with it. But, for God's sake, don't expect me to run away from it when—"

"You promised, John." It was all she could say.

"I said I wouldn't put on a gun against anybody! I never said I wouldn't defend myself! Can't you see there's a difference?"

"This isn't just anybody!" she said vehemently. "This is a boy who hasn't got a chance against you!"

"I make it that way?" he asked. "Did I tell him to challenge me?"

"It doesn't matter who challenged who! You can't fight him, that's all!"

"Julia, I'm going to fight him."

The words seemed to come from the very depth of her fear and her fury; they fell from her lips slowly and clearly.

"John Benton," she said, "if you draw your gun against that boy, it'll be murder. *Murder!*"

He looked at her colorless face a long time before turning away to the stove and saying, "That's right. It will be."

She stood there shivering, watching his steady hand pour coffee into the cup. He took the cup and walked out of the room and she listened to the sound of his boots moving through the house, then the sound of him sinking down on their bed.

Her eyes suddenly closed and she flung a hand across them as a wracking sob broke in her throat. Stumbling through a haze of tears, she moved to the table and sank down, her head falling forward on her arms, her body lurching with great, hopeless sobs.

She was conscious of the clock striking two.

Then, outside, there was a sound of turning wheels and thudding hooves. She straightened up with a gasp, a look of shocked surprise on her face. Hastily, she reached into her dress pocket and drew out a handkerchief. She dabbed at her cheeks and eyes as she stood up and hurried to the door.

It's them, the terrifying thought came suddenly. They said three but it was only a trick and they were coming at two to catch John by surprise.

Then, in the doorway, she stopped and stared out blankly at the small woman getting out of a rig with hurried, nervous movements.

Julia stood rooted there as the woman came up to her.

"Your husband hasn't gone yet, has he?" the woman asked quickly.

"No," Julia said, not understanding. "No, he—"

"Thank God," Jane Coles said fervently, then stood there awkwardly, clutching the shawl to herself.

"Come in," Julia said, feeling her heart start to throb in slow, heavy beats. What was Mrs. Coles doing there? For a second, Julia had the wild hope that the fight was canceled and Mrs. Coles was the one they'd sent with the message. But that didn't make sense and she knew it.

As she stepped aside to let the small woman enter, John appeared in the other doorway, tensed as though he were expecting the same thing Julia had expected.

When he saw Robby's mother, the tenseness left his face and was replaced by a look of startled surprise. He didn't say anything as Mrs. Coles came over to him.

"Mister Benton," she said.

He nodded once. "Missus Coles," he replied, looking down at the small frailty of her.

"I—" She said. "I . . . wanted to—to—"

"Yes?" he said.

There was silence for a terrible moment, a silence that seemed, suddenly, as if it would be permanent, holding them all fast in it.

But then Mrs. Coles' faint voice spoke. "I . . . came about . . . about the fight," she said, nervously.

Benton tightened a little but still he didn't understand. He looked down at her with confused eyes. "I . . ." he started and then waited.

"My boy is . . ." Mrs. Coles started and then suddenly it all came rushing out. "Oh, Mister Benton, don't hurt him! Don't hurt my boy!"

Benton jerked back the upper part of his body as if someone had struck him across the face; his expression was one of stunned shock.

"Don't . . ." he started to repeat her words, then broke off shakily.

"Please, Mister Benton, please. I'm begging you as

his mother. Don't hurt him! He's just a boy. He doesn't know anything about g-guns or-or fighting. He's just a boy, Mister Benton, just a boy!"

Benton's lips twitched as he sought for proper words but couldn't find them.

"Mister Benton, I beg of you," Jane Coles went on brokenly and Julia shuddered, hearing in the older woman's voice a repetition of her own words to Mrs. Coles' husband a little over an hour before.

"Missus Coles, I . . ." Benton said nervously. "I . . . I didn't ask for this fight. I didn't—"

"I don't know anything about that," Jane Coles said miserably. "All I know is I love my boy and I'll die if anything happens to him."

"But Missus Coles, I just told you I—"

"Oh, please, Mister Benton, *please*." There were tears now, running down the small woman's cheeks, and her hands were shaking helplessly before her.

"What do you want me to do?" he asked her quietly as if he really thought she could give him an answer.

She sobbed helplessly, staring at him, unable to see any part of the situation but the threat to her boy.

"Missus Coles, what do you want me to *do*?" Benton asked again, his voice rising. "Just wait for your son to *kill* me?"

"He wouldn't, he wouldn't!" she sobbed. "He's a good boy, there's nothing mean in him. He wouldn't hurt anyone, Mister Benton, not anyone!"

"Missus Coles, your own husband told me to be in town by three o'clock or Robby would come after me. What choice does that give me?"

She had no answer, only frightened looks and sobs.

"Missus Coles, I don't want this thing any more than you do. I have a life too, you know. I have my wife and I have this ranch. I'm happy here, Missus Coles, I don't want to die any more than Robby does. But I'm being forced into this, can't you see that?"

"Don't hurt him, Mister Benton," she pleaded. "Don't hurt him, please don't hurt my boy."

Benton started to say something, then, abruptly, he turned on his heel and walked away from her. At the door to the inner hall, he turned.

"You'd better go home and talk to your husband, Missus Coles," he said grimly. "He's the only one that can stop this fight now. I'm sorry but my hands are tied."

"Mister Benton!"

But he was gone. Julia moved quickly to the trembling woman and put an arm around her.

"You've got to stop him, Missus Benton," Jane Coles begged. "You've got to stop him from hurting my boy."

Julia looked at her with a hopeless expression on her face. Then she sighed and spoke.

"You'd better go see your husband, Missus Coles," she said softly. "He *is* the only one who can stop it now. I'm ... I'm sorry." She fought down the sob. "You ... don't know how sorry I am."

"But he won't listen to me," Mrs. Coles sobbed. "He just won't listen to me."

Julia closed her eyes and turned away.

"Please go," she muttered thickly. "That's all there is. Believe me, that's all there is."

When Jane Coles had climbed into her rig like a dying woman and driven away, Julia walked slowly into the silence of the bedroom. John was sitting on the bed, his head slumped forward, his hands hanging loosely and motionlessly between his legs. On the bedside table his coffee stood cold and untouched.

He didn't even look up as she came into the room. Only when she sat down beside him did he turn his head slowly and meet her glance. His eyes were lifeless.

Then his head dropped forward again and his voice, as he spoke, was husky and without strength.

"I'm tired, ma," he said. "I'm awful tired."

Slowly, her arm moved around his back and she pressed her face into his shoulder.

"I know," she murmured. Her eyes closed and she felt warm tears running slowly down her cheeks. "I know."

Chapter Twenty-eight

He tried to sit down and rest but there seemed to be a spring in him that coiled tight every time he sat down. First the tension would affect his hands and feet, making them twitch. Then his shoulders would twist with a tortured restlessness, his hands would close into white-knuckled fists, and the turbulence in him would show in his eyes as a haunted flickering.

Then, abruptly, he'd be on his feet again, pacing back and forth on the sitting room rug, the fist of one hand pounding slowly and methodically into the palm of the other. His gaze would flit about the room from one object to another as though he had lost something and was making a rapid, futile search for it. His boots scuffed and thudded on the thick rug and there was no rest in him.

Robby dropped down onto the couch for the twenty-seventh time and sat there feeling the coils drawing in again. His chest rose and fell with quick, agitated breaths as he stared at his hands.

On the bottom step in the hall, his brother sat peering between the bannisters, the freckles on his face standing out like cinnamon sprinkled on milk. He watched Robby start to his feet again and begin pacing.

"When you gonna fight him?" he asked.

Robby didn't answer. He breathed as if there were an obstruction in his throat.

"Robby?"

"Three o'clock. L-eave me alone."

"Where, Robby? Are ya goin' out to his ranch?"

Robby's teeth gritted together as he stopped and looked out the window at the street.

This was Armitas Street, Kellville, Texas. It was his town, it had dozens of houses and hundreds of people and stores and stables and horses and life and future. Yet in—how long?; he glanced nervously at the hall clock and saw that it was five minutes after two.

In less than an hour it might all be taken from him.

Might be? What question was there? He couldn't draw a gun like John Benton, he couldn't fire half as quickly or accurately. He'd never even gotten the hang of cocking the hammer after each shot; he'd always fumbled at it.

He jammed his teeth together to stop the chattering. Oh, good God, he was going to die! The thought impaled him on a spear of frozen terror. He jammed his eyes shut and felt a violent shudder run down his back.

"Robby, where are ya gonna?"

"I said, leave me alone," Robby muttered.

"What did you say, Robby?"

"I said—! Oh . . . *never mind.* Shut up, will ya?"

"But where are ya gonna fight him?"

"In the square! Now will ya leave me alone!"

Jimmy sat staring at his pacing brother. He wished he was big enough to fight somebody with a gun like Robby. Maybe he could fight his father.

The vision crossed his mind with a pleasant tread— him and his father facing each other in the square, guns buckled to their waists. *Awright pa, fill yer hand!* Sudden drawing, the blast of pistol fire, his father clutching at his chest, him re-holstering his pistol and running to his mother. *It's all right now, ma, it's all right. I killed him. He's dead now and he can't hurt us no more.*

His eyes focused on Robby who was on the couch again. He looked over at the clock.

"There isn't much time," he said, helpfully.

Robby forced his lips together, eyes staring at the floor.

"Robby, there isn't much time."

Robby stood up with a lurching movement and went to the window again. He stood there tensely, punching slowly at his cupped palm. Jimmy sat there listening to the dead smacking sound of the fist hitting the palm.

"Robby, there isn't much—"

"Will you *shut up*!" Robby screamed at him, whirling, his face contorted with rage. Jimmy felt a sudden jolting in his stomach and drew back from the bannister quickly.

"I was only—"

"Get out of here!" his brother yelled. "I'm sick of lookin' at ya!"

Jimmy sat there rigidly, thinking how much Robby looked like his father when he was mad.

Robby started for him. "I said—get outta here," he warned, his voice a strange, unnatural sound.

Jimmy pushed up to his feet and ran up the steps, a sudden dryness in his mouth. At the head of the stairs, he stopped and glanced back. Robby hadn't come out into the hall; he could hear him down in the sitting room, pacing again.

Slowly, he settled on the top step and looked down the staircase. He wished he could wear a gun like Robby.

In the sitting room, Robby jumped up from the couch as a thudding of horses' hooves sounded outside. It's *him*—the words exploded in his mind as he ran for the window, his heart like a frenziedly beaten drum. He felt his legs almost buckle as he moved and he grunted in shock as he caught his balance.

There was no horse in the street. Robby drew back from the window with a frightened sucking in of breath. Did Benton ride into the backyard, was he going to *trap* him? Robby dashed for the table and, with nerveless fingers, jerked the Colt from its holster and backed away, his eyes wide with apprehension.

The back door slammed shut and there was a heavy clumping of boots in the kitchen. No, it couldn't be Benton, he wouldn't come in like that. It was his father, it *had* to be his father. He mustn't let his father see him like this, shivering, standing here with his pistol out-thrust and shaking in his hand. But what if it *was* Benton? Oh God, oh God, I *can't*!—he thought, choking on a repressed sob.

"Where are you, sir?" he heard his father's voice then and, hastily, he put the pistol down on the table and sat down.

"I'm, I'm . . ." he began, then braced himself. "*Here*, father," he said, not realizing how loudly his voice rang out in the house.

Matthew Coles entered the room, carrying a box with him.

"Where is your mother?" he asked.

"I . . . I don't know," Robby said, still sitting there, feeling as if a great weight were settling on him.

"Well, did she go out?"

"Y-yes," Robby faltered. "She . . . she just went out in the . . . rig."

"In the rig?" Matthew Coles said in displeased surprise. Robby didn't reply. He watched his father put the box on the table.

"Well, we'll settle that later," Matthew Coles said grimly. "There are more important things to be discussed now."

He opened the box and took out the pistol in it.

"I've brought you that new Colt," he told Robby. "Since you seem to have some difficulty with hammering. The double action in this model should take care of that. I don't believe you'll need more than two shots, will you."

The last sentence was not spoken as a question.

Robby watched as his father broke open the cylinder and spun it. He heard his father's grunt and then watched him break open the seal on a new box of cartridges. Carefully, Matthew Coles inserted a cartridge into each chamber, then spun the cylinder again. He looked into the barrel from the back, then grunted again, satisfied. Jerking his hand, he snapped the barrel back into place and spun the cylinder with one thumb.

"Yes," he said. "Yes, that will do fine."

He slid the Colt into Robby's holster and forgot about it. Pulling out a chair, he sat across from his son.

"Now," he said, "as to Benton's mode of fighting. I've spoken to several men who claim to have seen him fight once in Trinity City. According to them, he wears his pistol—a Colt-Walker single action, I might add—wears it on his left hip, stock forward, using a cross draw. Furthermore," he went on, "there is reason to believe he's very much out of practice. After all, he's been away from it a long time."

I've never been near it—the words moved across Robby's brain but he didn't speak them. He sat staring at his father, his eyes unblinking, his entire body feeling numbed and dead.

"These men further claim that Benton never fires at a distance of less than thirty feet. So that, I believe you may be able to seize an advantage over him by drawing your weapon at a greater distance. Your accuracy is good enough for that; especially with the better rifling in this—" he gesture toward the gun in the holster, "—weapon."

Robby swallowed the heavy lump in his throat. No, I'm sorry, he thought, I'm not going to do it. But, again, he said nothing. He sat stiffly, listening to his father plan his life away while, under the table, his nails dug into his palms without him feeling it.

"I believe you'll find much less in this battle than you expect, sir," Matthew Coles went on confidently. "John Benton has been away from gunplay a long while. Furthermore, I think we've seen ample evidence that he's lost his nerve. In particular, his attempts to back out of this meeting. Then, of course, there was the time he refused, point-blank, to aid the men of our town in that posse. Yes—" Matthew Coles nodded once, "—it's clear that the man is no longer what he once was."

Robby's throat was petrifying. It came slowly, starting at the bottom and rising as if someone poured cement in his mouth and he kept swallowing it. He shuddered, his hands twitching in his lap.

"As to having the issue settled in the town rather than out of it, well, I believe you can understand that. This entire matter can be settled only when the people of the town see that you are willing to defend the honor of your intended bride. They must see it; for the sake of all concerned."

Silence a moment. Matthew Coles drew out his watch and pressed in the catch. The thinly wrought gold cover sprang open and he looked calmly down at the face. His head nodded once with a curt motion and he closed the watch and put it back into his pocket.

"It's time," he said, looking at his son with a sort of pride. "Shall we go, sir?"

Robby didn't answer. There was something cold and terrible crawling in his stomach as he stared at his father.

"Sir?" asked Matthew Coles.

"I—"

His father stood up with one, unhesitant motion. "Are you ready, sir?" he asked like a general asking his troops if they were ready for suicidal battle.

Robby found himself standing up even though he didn't want to. He started for the door on numbed legs.

"Your weapon, sir," Matthew Coles said, his voice slightly acidulous.

"Father, I—"

"Put on your weapon, sir," Matthew Coles said, calmly.

I've got to tell you!—Robby thought in agony of speechless terror. But he found himself moving back to the table on legs that felt like blocks of stone, he saw his hands reaching for the belt.

It weighed a hundred pounds; his shaking hands could hardly lift it.

"Come, sir, there's no time to waste. We want to be there before three."

Robby put the gunbelt around his back and fumbled at the buckle. As he did, he stared down at the butt of the new Colt and thought about drawing it against Benton. He thought of walking across the square toward the tall ex-Ranger, of trying to outdraw a man who had killed thirteen outlaws; thirteen men who, themselves, could have outdrawn Robby without trying.

Thirteen!

He couldn't help it. His fingers went limp suddenly and the unfastened belt and holster thumped loudly on the rug.

"Be careful, will you, a—"

Matthew Coles broke off suddenly his mouth gaping as he stood there staring with incredulous eyes at the tears that were scattering across Robby's cheeks and listening to the hoarse, shaking sobs his son was trying, in vain, to control.

"What is the meaning of . . . ?" Again, he couldn't finish. His head moved forward on his shoulders and he peered intently into the twisted face of his son, staring at the trembling lips, the wide, glistening eyes, the quivering chin.

"What is the meaning of this, sir?" he asked, heatedly. "Explain yourself this very—"

"I-I-I c-can't, I *can't*, father! Please, p-lease. I can't. I . . . j-j-just can't."

"What?" The word came slowly from Matthew Coles' lips, rising with anger.

"I can't, I c-can't. He'll kill me, he'll k-*ill* me, father. I'm a-f-*fraid*." Robby didn't even try to brush away the tears that laced across his cheeks and dripped from his chin and jaw.

"Can't, sir?" Matthew Coles was having trouble adjusting to this. "Can't? What are you saying to me? There is no question of—"

"I won't *do* it!" Robby cried suddenly, his voice cracking. "I *won't*! I'm not gonna die f-for nothing!"

His father seemed to swell up before him and Robby stepped back, nervously, a rasping sob in his throat. Matthew Coles looked at him with terrible eyes, his hands twitching at his sides.

"Pick up your weapon, sir," he said in a slow, menacing voice.

"No . . . n-no," Robby muttered fearfully, his chest jerking with uncontrolled breaths.

"*Pick up your weapon.*"

"No. No, I can't, father, I *can't*!"

"You have given your word, sir," Matthew Coles said, his voice quivering as he repressed the volcano of fury within himself. "You have promised to defend the honor of your intended bride. Everyone is waiting, sir, everyone expects it. Pick up your weapon and we'll say no more of this."

Robby backed away another step, shaking his head with little, twitching movements. "No," he muttered. "No, I . . ."

"Pick up your weapon!" his father shouted, his face growing purple with released fury. He took two quick steps across the rug and clamped his rigid fingers on Robby's arm. Robby winced as the fingers dug into his flesh. He stood there staring at his father, his head still jerking back and forth, his lips moving as if he were trying to speak but couldn't.

"You cannot back out of this! This is something you have to do, do you understand! It's a matter of honor! If you do this thing to me, there will be no place in this house for you! Do you understand *that*!"

"F-f-father, I—"

"*Are you going to pick up that gun and come with me!*"

Robby tried to answer, to explain but terror welled over him again and he started to cry harder, his shoulders twitching helplessly, his throat clutched with breathless sobs.

"*No!*" he cried out and his head snapped to the side suddenly as Matthew Coles' broad palm drove stunningly against his cheek. The room seemed to blacken for a moment and Robby stumbled back, clutching at his cheek with one hand, his eyes dumb with shock.

"Coward!" his father screamed at him. "Coward, coward, *coward*! My own son a coward!"

Matthew Coles lurched away toward the hall, his face a mask of near-mad rage. At the doorway, he twisted around.

"When I come back tonight I want you gone! Do you hear me, *gone*! I don't want a coward in my house! I won't have one! Do you understand!"

Robby stood there, shivering without control, staring with blank eyes at his father.

A moment more his father looked at him.

"Swine," Matthew Coles said through clenched teeth. "Filthy little coward. You should have been a girl, a little girl cooking in the kitchen—hanging on your mother's apron strings."

Then Matthew Coles was gone in the hall and Robby heard the front door jerked open.

"By tonight!" he heard his father shout from there. "If you're still in my house then, I'll throw you out!"

The door slammed deafeningly, shaking the house. Robby slumped down on the couch and covered his face with shaking hands. Trying to fight off the deep sobs only made them worse. He couldn't control anything. He sat there trembling helplessly, hearing his father gallop away outside, the sound of the gelding's hooves drowning out the noise of the turning wheels.

Suddenly, Robby looked up and caught his breath.

Jimmy was standing on the bottom step, looking at him. Robby felt himself grow rigid as he looked at his younger brother. He couldn't take his eyes off Jimmy's face and couldn't help recognizing the look of withdrawal and disappointed shame there. He opened his mouth as if to speak but couldn't. He didn't even hear the back door shut.

He stood up nervously and walked on shaky legs to where the gunbelt was. Bending over, he picked it up and held it in his hand, seeing, from the corners of his eyes, that Jimmy was still there. It's true—the words lanced at him—it's true, I am a coward, I *am!*

That was when his mother came in.

She stopped for an instant in the hallway, her eyes on Jimmy. Then she looked into the sitting room. When she saw the dazed, hurt look on Robby's face, she started toward him.

"Darling, what *is* it?" she asked, hurrying across the rug, her arms outstretched to him.

Robby stepped back. His mother rushing to embrace him, in his mind the lashing words of his father—*You should have been a girl, a little girl cooking in the kitchen, hanging on your mother's—*

"Oh, my darling, what happened?"

It was the sound in her voice that did it; that sound of a mother speaking to her little boy who she never wants to grow up and be a man.

"No!" he said in a strangled voice, suddenly twisting away from her arms and running toward the hall, the gunbelt clutched in his cold hand.

"Robby!"

He didn't answer. He saw the face of his younger brother rush by in a blur and then he was flying down the hall and into the kitchen, the frightened cries of his mother following him. He was on the porch, jumping down the steps and running into the stable where his horse was already saddled.

As he galloped out of the stable, his mother rushed

out onto the porch, one thin arm raised, her eyes dumb with terror.

"No, Robby!" she screamed, all the agony of her life trembling in the words.

As he started down Armitas Street for the square, Robby began buckling on the gun.

Chapter Twenty-nine

*T*wo *fifteen.* She stood in the leaden heat of the sun, shivering fitfully while she watched the shape of her husband dwindle away. She stayed there until he was gone from her sight. Then, slowly, with the tread of a very old and very tired woman, she walked back to the house.

She shuddered as she stepped into the relative coolness of the kitchen and her eyes moved slowly around the room as if she were searching for something.

In the middle of clearing the table, she suddenly pushed aside the stack of dishes and sank down heavily on a chair. She sat there, shivering still, feeling the waves of coldness run through her body. We'll have to move now—the thought assailed her—we can't possibly stay here with a murder on our conscience; we just can't.

Her right forefinger traced a straggly and invisible pattern on the rough table top and her unblinking eyes watched the finger moving.

Suddenly, her head jerked up and she felt her heartbeat catch. A horse coming in.

Julia pushed up with a muttering sound of excitement in her throat. He was coming back; he wasn't going into town! Her footsteps clicked rapidly across the kitchen floor and she jerked open the top half of the Dutch door.

It was like being drained of all her energy in an instant. Dumbly, she stood there, watching Merv Linken as he rode over to the bunkhouse, reined up, and dismounted. When he'd gone in, she turned away from the door slowly, unable to control the awful sinking in her stomach.

A moment later, she was running across the hard earth toward the bunkhouse, her blond hair fluttering across her temples.

Merv looked up in surprise as he bandaged his right wrist.

"Ma'm?" he asked.

She stood panting in the open doorway. "Will you hitch up the buckboard for me, Merv?" she asked breathlessly.

"Why . . . sure, Miz Benton," he said.

"What, what happened to your wrist?" she asked vaguely.

"Snagged it on some barbed wire," he said. "It's nothin'."

"Oh." She nodded. "Will . . . you do it for me right away, Merv?" she asked. "I have to get into—"

From the way the skin tightened over his leathery face, Julia realized suddenly that he knew.

"I just passed him," Merv said grimly. "He didn't say nothin' to me. Nothin' at all. Didn't even look at me."

Abruptly, he tore off the end of the clean rag he was bandaging his wrist with and started for the door without another question.

"I'll have her ready for you in a jiffy," he told her.

Ten minutes later, she was driving out of the ranch on the lurching, rattling buckboard, headed for Kellville.

For her husband.

Chapter Thirty

It was like some endless nightmare. She'd keep moving into the hall, past the clock and over to the head of the stairs; but, every time she did, her aunt would be down in the sitting room, talking to her mother. Louisa would come back along the hall rug, past the clock, and into her room once again. It happened that way again and again, always the same except for one thing. Every time she passed the clock, it was a different time. *Two ten—two fifteen—two twenty-one—two twenty-seven—*

Oh, dear God! She stood shaking at the head of the steps, wanting to scream, her cold hands clutching at the bannister. She had to get out, she *had* to! Only a little more than thirty minutes were left now. She bit her lower lip until it hurt and her breast shook with unresolved sobs.

I'll tell Aunt Agatha, I'll tell her I lied, I'll tell her to stop the fight. I have to, I just have to! And she'd go down one step, meaning to rush downstairs and tell everything and save Robby.

But, after one downward step, she'd freeze and be unable to go any farther. She'd never been able to talk to her aunt in her life. Her aunt was remote from her, a bony-faced, dark-garbed stranger. Tell *her* that she'd lied? Tell *her* that she was in love with John Benton and had made believe that . . .

She backed up the step again, lips shaking, tears forcing their way from her eyes and dribbling down her pale cheeks. She hurried back to her room, looking at the clock as she passed. Before she reached the door, she heard the tinny resonance of the clock chiming the half hour. In thirty minutes.

Thirty *minutes*!

She stood alone in her room, looking around desperately for the answer. She had to tell someone—but first of all she had to get out of the house.

She moved to the window quickly. Could she climb down the trellis? No, she'd fall and hurt herself. And, even if she managed to do it, surely they'd hear her climbing down.

A whimpering started in her throat and she turned restlessly from the window. But I have to do something! The thought filled her with terror. She couldn't just let Robby die!

She ran to the door, thinking she might climb down from her mother's window in back. But there was no ivy trellis in back, she suddenly remembered. She'd have to jump then. But it was too high—she'd kill herself. The whimper rose. Oh . . . no, *no*. Oh, God, help me to stop it—please, please . . .

The minute hand was moving away from the six now. Louisa stared at it with sick fascination. I can see it moving now, she thought dizzily, they say you can't really see a clock hand but I can—

Oh, God, it's going to the seven! I have to *do* something!

She ran to the head of the stairs. Her stomach was tightening, she was starting to feel sick. I have to do something, I have to stop it, I *have* to. She pressed her shaking hands together, staring down the steps toward the front door.

I have to!

Suddenly, she felt herself running down the stairs, making no effort to be quiet, her shoes thudding quickly on the carpeted steps.

Before she reached the bottom step, Aunt Agatha came hurrying from the sitting room.

"Where do you think you're going?" she demanded.

"I have to stop it," Louisa gasped.

"Stop it?" her aunt said, questioningly. "I don't see what—"

"Aunt Agatha, it's my fault—mine! Please tell them to stop. I didn't mean to . . ."

She stood there trembling, thinking—there, it's said, I've *said* it and I don't care as long as Robby is safe.

"Louisa, go to your room," Aunt Agatha said.

Louisa didn't understand. "But I said—"

"I heard what you said."

"But we have to stop it!"

"Stop what?"

"The fight!"

Aunt Agatha's lips pressed together. "I *thought* you'd found out about it," she said. "If you'd remained in your room as I told you, this wouldn't have—"

"But, Aunt Agatha, we have to stop it!"

"I'm afraid that's not possible."

"But it's my fault, Aunt Agatha! I made up the story; I didn't tell the truth!"

Aunt Agatha's eyes closed a moment. "I understand, Louisa," she said calmly. "It shows you have a good heart. But I'm afraid it's too late now."

Louisa didn't understand. She stared at her aunt incredulously. "But . . ." she murmured.

"I'm sure we appreciate your wish to prevent violence, Louisa. However, there is no alterna—"

"But it's *my fault!*" Louisa burst out, tears springing from under her eyelids. "I made up the story! John Benton never even *spoke* to me!"

"Go to your room, Louisa."

"Aunt Agatha!"

"Louisa, this instant . . ."

Louisa couldn't believe it was true. She stared at her aunt dazedly, feeling her heart beat in great, rocking jolts.

Abruptly, she turned to her mother who had come into the hall. "Mother, you have to—"

"Lou-*isa!*" Agatha Winston's voice was metallic. "That will do."

"But you have to—"

"Go to your room, I said!"

"You're not going to—?" Louisa began in a faint voice.

"Louisa, if I have to say another word, you'll remain in this house for a month," Agatha Winston stated.

"Darling, please don't make it worse," her mother begged.

Louisa backed away, her eyes stricken with horror at what she'd done.

Then, suddenly, she lurched for the front door and jerked it open. Before her surprised aunt could jump forward to grab her, Louisa had run out onto the porch.

"Lou-*isa!*" Aunt Agatha's sharp cry followed her as she fled down the path and flung open the picket gate.

"Oh, my dear—please," her mother pleaded in a voice that no one heard.

Agatha Winston ran as far as the gate, her lean face masked with outraged surprise. There, she stopped and watched Louisa running frantically down Davis Street toward the square.

In the hallway, she put on her bonnet with quick, agitated motions. "She's lost her mind," she muttered, paying no attention to her distraught sister. "She's taken leave of her senses. Made it up, in-*deed!* Does she think a *lie* is going to stop this fight?"

She hurried from the house, leaving behind a weeping Mrs. Harper, standing in the hallway, trembling and thinking if only her dear husband were alive.

Twenty-two minutes to three.

Chapter Thirty-one

It was exactly twenty minutes to three when the Reverend Omar Bond came out of the white-steepled church on the way to his adjoining house and saw John Benton riding slowly up St. Virgil Street toward the square.

"Oh, Mister Benton," he called, stepping out into the street.

Benton glanced over, then when he'd seen who it was, he tugged a little at the barbit, reining the bay to a slow halt. The Reverend Bond walked up to the horse, smiling up at Benton.

"Afternoon, Reverend," Benton said to him.

"Good afternoon, Mister Benton," Bond answered. "My apologies for stopping you. I just wanted to find out how things went yesterday."

Benton looked down in surprise at the dark-suited man. "You don't know?" he asked.

The smile faded. "Know?" the Reverend said, disturbedly.

"I'm to meet Robby Coles in the square at three o'clock," Benton told him.

"Meet him," Bond repeated blankly.

Then it struck him. "Oh, dear Lord, no!" he said in a shocked voice. "In *one day*?"

Benton didn't say anything. He drew out his watch and looked at it, his expression unchanged.

"But it must be stopped," Bond said.

Benton's mouth tightened. "It's no use talkin' to anyone, Reverend," he said. "Nobody wants to listen. They want what they want and that's it."

"Oh, *no*, Mister Benton," Bond said, arguing desperately. "This meeting must not take place."

"It's too late, Reverend," Benton said quietly. "There's not much more than fifteen minutes left."

"Dear God, it *must* be stopped," said the Reverend in a tight, unaccepting voice. He raised his hand to shade his eyes from the sun as he looked up at Benton. "Come with me to Louisa Harper's home," he asked. "She will surely confess when she hears that there is a life at stake."

Benton looked restless. "Reverend," he said, "I been all through this. Yesterday I came in like you asked. I tried to talk reason with these people. And this mornin' both Julia and I came in. The girl's aunt wouldn't even let my wife in the house. Nobody would listen."

"But surely they don't realize—"

"Reverend, they *do* realize," Benton said. "It doesn't matter to them. They don't care, they don't *want* to believe I didn't do what they said. They want blood, Reverend." Benton's lips tightened for a fraction of a second. "They'll get blood," he said.

"Oh, no . . . *no*."

"I have to go, Reverend," Benton said.

"The sheriff, then!"

"He's out of town, Reverend. I'm sorry. I have to go now."

"Is there *no* one?"

"No one, Reverend."

"There is you, Mister Benton. I beg of you to reconsider."

"Reverend, I have to be in the square by three o'clock," Benton told him firmly. "I'm sorry." The coldness left his voice then. "Believe me, I'm sorry, Reverend. I didn't ask for this thing. I did everything I could to stop it, I swear to that. But—" his head shook slowly, "it's no use."

"I'll go to Louisa," Bond said quickly. "I'll tell her. She *must* confess her lie!"

Benton said nothing but his gaze moved restlessly up St. Virgil Street toward the square.

"Mister Benton, can't you hold this thing off? Can't you prevent it from happening until I can reach the girl?"

Benton shifted in the saddle. "Reverend, they said three o'clock," he said. "I'll do what I can but . . ." He shrugged with a hopeless gesture.

"Then . . ." Bond looked carefully at the tall man, his mind a twisting rush of conflicts. "Mister Benton I . . . I know nothing of these things, nothing. But . . . well, you have a reputation for . . ." he struggled for the words, ". . . for accuracy and . . . and quickness with your . . . your weapon."

Benton looked down expressionlessly at the churchman. "What do you mean?" he asked guardedly.

"I know this may be unreasonable but . . . isn't it possible for you to—to merely *wound* young Coles? Even if you cannot avoid the meeting in time, couldn't you end it without taking his life?"

Benton looked down with a tense expression.

"Reverend . . . you don't know what you're asking me." He rubbed a hand across his sweat-streaked brow and wiped it on his Levi's. "Beggin' your pardon but . . . well, you just don't know what a gunslingin' is like. It's not somethin' that . . . that *lasts*. It's not somethin' you can play with. It happens too fast, Reverend, too damn fast."

Bond stood there, looking up blankly at the worried face of John Benton.

"And . . . well, besides that," Benton said grudgingly, as if he felt he must be understood, "I've been away from it a long time. I haven't drawn a gun on anybody in more than eight years—and gunslingin' is somethin' you have to keep up with or you lose the touch."

He gritted his teeth, seeing that he wasn't getting across to Bond.

"How do I know how fast Robby is?" he asked. "What if I go into this meanin' to crease him and then he outdraws me before I even get the chance?"

"But, surely . . ."

"No, I just can't take that chance, Reverend," Benton said. "If I was in practice—yes, I might do it but . . . not now."

He hesitated, then started in again, his voice rising. "Reverend, hittin' an arm or a leg in the split second a gunslingin' takes is hard enough t'do when a man's with it every day. But I been away from it over *eight years*." He shook his head. "I just can't do it, Reverend, I . . . just can't. I want to live too—just like him."

"Well, will you try to keep the fight from starting until I can reach Louisa Harper then?" Bond asked in a hurried, anxious voice.

"Reverend, I . . ." Benton exhaled heavily. "I'll try," he said. "But you'd better hurry."

He tugged at the reins then and the bay moved off toward the square.

Bond rushed up the path to his house and into the hall, his eyes seeking for the clock as he entered. Two forty-seven.

Thirteen minutes.

"Oh, dear Lord," he muttered in a choked voice as he headed for the kitchen.

"Omar, what is—?" his wife started to ask as he dashed toward the back door.

"No time!" he cried and then was gone.

When she appeared on the porch, he was trying feverishly to get the bridle on their gray mare and attach the animal to the rig.

"Omar, what is it?" she asked, anxiously.

"Benton and young Coles going to fight in the square at three!" he gasped, his fingers fumbling at the leather.

"Oh, no," Mrs. Bond murmured.

"I'm going to Louisa Harper's house to try and stop it!" Bond told her.

A minute and a half later, he was whipping the mare out the alley and the rig was groaning as it turned onto St. Virgil Street and headed for Davis Street.

Mrs. Bond went back into the kitchen, shaken by the sight of her husband so upset, so white.

When the front doorbell jangled suddenly in the stillness, Mrs. Bond dropped the wooden spoon she was stirring with. Before the clatter had died in her ears, she was in the hallway, moving on skirt-whipping legs toward the door.

Her eyes widened as she saw who it was.

"Where's the Reverend?" Louisa Harper gasped.

Mrs. Bond knew about the affair and a succession of emotions jolted through her as she stared at the flushed, perspiring face of the young girl—shock first, then confusion, then excited resolve, then a sudden dread as she realized that Omar had said *three o'clock.*

"Quickly, child," she said. "The story you told. It wasn't true, was it?"

Louisa draw back a little, staring at Mrs. Bond with a startled expression. "Where's the Reverend?" she asked in a thin, frightened voice.

"Child, he's gone!" Mrs. Bond answered quickly. "He went to see you. We must hurry! That story—it wasn't true was it?"

Louisa still stared, her chest jerking with laboring breath.

"Child, there's no time! There are only minutes left!"

"No!" Louisa sobbed. "They have to stop! I didn't tell the truth. John B-Benton didn't speak to me."

"Will you repeat that to Robby Coles?" Mrs. Bond asked desperately, glancing toward the clock. *Two fifty-one.*

Louisa bit her shaking lips and stood there panting, the hair straggling across her forehead.

"Child, for the love of God! Will you repeat it?"

"Yes!" Louisa burst out. "Yes, I will, I will!"

"Quickly then!" Mrs. Bond grabbed her hand. "We'll have to run!"

They started down the path, the two of them, rushing for the square. In the empty hall the minute hand edged toward the eleven. *Eight minutes—seven minutes, fifty-nine seconds—seven minutes, fifty-eight seconds—seven minutes, fifty-seven . . .*

Chapter Thirty-two

He was tired. He tried to sit up straight in the saddle but he couldn't. His muscles ached; his arm muscles and the muscles in his shoulders and back—they all ached from digging and pushing the cows from the bog.

But that was only the immediate fatigue. There was the lack of sleep from the night before too. And all of that was only the surface of the endless undercurrent of exhaustion he'd felt since he'd bought the small ranch with his Ranger earnings and tried to make a going thing of it. Life in the Rangers hadn't prepared him for it. Life in the Rangers had been a hard one but more because it was dangerous than anything else. And danger didn't make the body ache with weariness.

He was near the square now. He took out his watch and opened it.

Seven minutes to three. He eased the bay over the side of the street and reined up. No point in leaving Socks anywhere near the square where a stray slug might hit him.

Benton dismounted and started tying up. He watched his tanned hands as they wound the leather rein twice around the rough wood of the hitching bar, then looped it under. His hands didn't shake but that didn't mean anything; that was just learned habit. He could be twisted in knots inside and none of it would show in his hands or his face. That was the way he was.

He finished tying up the horse now and stood there a moment, looking at Socks with a sad smile. There was a tightness around his lower stomach starting. It came to him as a sudden jolt that he was nervous.

He swallowed and patted the bay's muzzle.

"See you, churnhead," he said softly, then stooped down and moved under the hitching rack and stepped up onto the sidewalk.

He stood there, looking around. The street seemed to be deserted but he knew that people were watching him from their windows. From the corners of his eyes he noted the momentary flutter of a window shade across the street and his mouth tightened. He started walking for the square, his hands swinging in short, tense arcs at his sides.

About five minutes now, he thought. Robby would probably be in the square already, waiting with his father. Benton took a deep breath. He wished it was Matthew Coles he was meeting. That wouldn't bother him so much.

He tried not to think about it. He tried to convince himself that there was nothing he could do; that it really *was* out of his hands. He was defending himself, that was all.

But he knew it wasn't so. It was a lot more than that. He didn't want this fight, he didn't want it at all. Robby was just a kid. Julia had been right; he didn't want to believe it but there was nothing else he could do. It would be . . . *murder. John Benton, if you draw your gun against that boy* . . . He blinked and tried to drive away her words.

Now he saw the square. It was strange to see it so empty. The last time he'd seen an empty square was in Trinity City. That was the time Jack Kramer had been waiting for him. That one had been easy. He'd hated

Jack Kramer and he'd been in top condition. Kramer went down with two slugs in his chest before he'd even gotten a chance to draw his two Colts.

No use thinking of that now. This wasn't the same. He didn't hate Robby Coles, he didn't hate him at all. He felt sorry for—

No! He fought that off too. It didn't matter what he felt, he told himself, he was still fighting for his life. If he didn't get Robby, Robby would get him. It was as simple as that.

If only he could forget Julia, if only he didn't keep hearing what she'd said. *John Benton, if you draw your gun against that—*

He stopped abruptly and caught hold of himself. Drawing out his watch, he snapped open the cover. Three minutes. Well, there was no point in planning on Bond getting to the girl in time. Benton swallowed dryly. Did he dare wait and not be in the square at three? Maybe if he could stall a little longer, Bond might . . .

No. That was impossible too. They had said three and it was no use fighting himself. Maybe it was pointless, maybe even stupid but when three o'clock came, he had to be in the square. It was the way he was and there was no way to change it now.

He put the watch away and took out his pistol. Opening the cylinder, he took a cartridge from his belt and filled the empty chamber. One of these slugs—the thought came—is going to kill Robby Coles.

Or *was* it?

He shuddered as he slid the pistol into its holster and started walking again, his mud-caked boots thudding on the plank sidewalk. What kind of question was that? He didn't understand where it had come from. And yet it was true—he didn't know how fast Robby was. He'd never given it a thought; it just never seemed as if it were possible that . . .

And yet it was, of course. Benton felt a cold sinking

in his stomach. I've been away from it too long, he thought, I'm starting to worry about it. That's what happens when you're away too long.

He shoved the thought aside. How could Robby possibly outdraw him when all he did was work in a shop all day? No, he was going to die.

Benton's throat moved as he thought, once again, of Julia's words. And he wondered, as he approached the square, if it were possible to do what Bond had asked. At one time, it might have been simple. But he hadn't drawn on anyone in a long time. Could he possibly . . .

His chest shuddered with forced breath. Too much thinking, he told himself angrily, too damned much thinking! He tried to blank his mind to all thought but one: There was an armed man in the square, waiting to kill him.

He stopped at the end of an alleyway that led to Taylor Street. He squinted toward the sun-drenched square. They'd expect him to come down St. Virgil Street because it led out of town to the trail.

Abruptly, he moved into the shaded length of the alley. Maybe he'd come out where they didn't expect him. They might not see him right away, it might put more distance between them. That might save a minute and give Bond a chance to get back with the girl. It was worth a try anyway.

He was halfway down the alley when the two of them entered it from the other end. The second they saw him, they froze in their tracks.

Benton didn't stop. He kept walking until he was fifteen feet from them, then he stopped. He paid no attention to Joe Sutton; his eyes were fastened to the stiff features of Dave O'Hara.

"Well?" he said.

O'Hara swallowed and tried not to move his hands.

"I told you if you ever saw me with a gun on, you could say it again," Benton told him.

O'Hara swallowed convulsively.

"What do you say, little boy?" Benton snapped. "I haven't got all day."

O'Hara's lips started shaking. His dark eyes stared petrified at Benton.

"All right, unbuckle your belt," Benton ordered.

"Huh?"

"You heard me."

With cold, shaking fingers, O'Hara fumbled at the buckle until it came loose. He let the whole belt drop to the ground with a crash.

"Pick it up," Benton told him, standing motionless, his hands hanging loosely at his sides.

O'Hara bent over obediently and picked up the belt.

"Now drop it in that trough," Benton told him.

O'Hara started to say something and then changed his mind. Biting his lip, he moved on unsteady legs to the trough while Joe Sutton watched incredulously, taking it all in.

"Drop it in."

The belt was released and it made a loud splash as it hit the water. They all heard it thump as it hit the bottom of the trough.

"You're not big enough for a gun yet, sonny," Benton said coldly. "Don't let me see you with one anymore."

His eyes shifted to Sutton and he looked at him a moment without saying anything.

He didn't have to say anything.

Without another word, he walked past the two of them and turned left at the end of the alley, a thin smile playing on his lips. *Flannel mouth*, he thought.

Then the smile was gone and he walked in long, regular strides until he'd reached the foot of Taylor Street.

John Benton stepped down from the sidewalk and walked out onto the edge of the square.

His eyes moved slowly around the edge of the square until they settled on the two figures far across from him, standing in front of their gunsmith shop.

Benton felt his heart start pumping heavily and he

pulled out his watch. Two seconds after three o'clock. He was on time.

He'd stand right there, the idea came. He wouldn't move; then it would take Robby longer to reach him and maybe Bond could get back in time to stop it.

He put his watch away and took a deep breath. Far across the square, Robby Coles left the side of his father and started walking slowly toward Benton.

Benton felt his fingers twitch and then felt that indicative tensing of his right arm muscles.

But it was different. A look of tense uncertainty flitted across his face. The heat of anger wasn't there, the confidence-inspiring knowledge that the man he was about to face deserved to die.

His heartbeat faltered. It's different, he thought, it's *different*. He hadn't even conceived it could be like this. It had always been so definite before, so clearly defined. He'd had a job to do and there had been a badge on his chest that gave him the permission to kill. And, deep inside he'd known that, if he killed, the man who died deserved no more.

Until the Grahams . . .

He almost backed away. There was a cold lacing of sweat across his brow and Julia's words hit him again. *It'll be murder. Murder!* His throat moved nervously and he began to look around for Bond. He had to get to the girl in time, he had to!

Desperately, he tried to tell himself it was self defense, he was forced into it. But he couldn't convince himself. And now his hands were shaking, something that had never happened before. Dear God, how could he fire on someone he had no reason to fire on?

He felt a shudder run down his back. *It'll be murder.* He blinked and brushed away the sweat drops that ran into his eyebrows and over his upper cheeks. One salty drop of it ran into his mouth. He clenched his teeth and looked across the square at the approaching figure of

Robby. How far away was he? A hundred yards? No, less, less.

He stood there rigidly, throat tightening as he watched Robby come closer. Go back, he thought suddenly, go *back*! Again his glance fled to all the street openings of the square, searching. Where was *Bond*!

His eyes shifted again. How far now? Seventy-five yards. No, it wasn't that far.

Should he turn and leave? What could they do? By the time they found him, Louisa could be forced to tell the truth.

No. He couldn't do that, he knew he couldn't. It didn't matter how desperate he was not to fight Robby, he couldn't run. It just wasn't in him to run. But what was he going to—

All right! His face grew taut in the instant he made his decision and, with a slight lurch, he began walking across the wide square toward Robby.

There was no noise at all. It was so quiet, the sound of his boots pressing down on the earth sounded clearly. He walked slowly and unhesitantly, eyes focused on the approaching boy.

Now he could see Robby's face. It was tight and without expression of any kind—a white mask of rigidly held determination.

Sixty yards now, fifty-nine, eight, seven. Benton felt his arm muscles tightening, readying. I've got to let him draw first, he ordered himself, *I've got to let him draw first*.

His boot heels crunched over the hot, dry ground, his eyes were fastened to the hands of Robby Coles.

Fifty yards.

Benton suddenly tensed as Robby's hand flew up to his pistol and he fought down the instinct of muscles to draw at the same time.

The roar of the Colt cracked a million jagged lines of sound in the silence of the square. Dirt kicked up two yards in front of Benton. Good God, what's wrong with him?—the question lanced across his mind. It was an easy shot.

He had his hand on his pistol butt just as the second blast of gunfire sent echoes rocking through the square. Dirt kicked up at his feet and he heard the slug whine ricocheting into the air.

The gun was in his hand then, suddenly. He stopped walking and twisted himself a half turn so he could extend his arm and aim. The third shot roared and he saw Robby's lips jerk back from clenched teeth as the bullet struck him in the right arm. He saw Robby's gun fall and hit the ground and, slowly, he lowered his arm.

Then he stiffened again, his breath catching. Robby had fallen to his knees and was trying to pick up the pistol, his face twisted with pain and terror.

The pistol fell from Robby's numbed right hand and, with a sob that Benton could hear, Robby grabbed at the Colt with his left hand. And, as Robby looked up, it seemed to Benton, in that instant, that he could see, in Robby's eyes, the same agonized dread he'd seen in Albert Graham's eyes just before he'd shot him.

Benton's shout filled the square.

"*Robby! Leave it alone!*"

But Robby had already thrown up the pistol, forced back the hammer and fired again. Benton heard the slug whistling by his right shoulder and, jerking up his pistol automatically, he thumbed back the hammer and fired.

The shot was too rushed, too shaken. The bullet only creased the edge of Robby's left arm and he was so numbed by fear that he didn't feel it. He jerked at the trigger and the silence was shattered again.

Benton staggered back with a startled grunt as though he'd been struck across the chest with a club. The Colt slipped from his suddenly lax fingers and, before it hit the ground, another slug drove into his chest, knocking him back further. With a sharp gasp, he fell to one knee, face dazed, dumbstruck eyes staring at the white-face boy who was sitting on the ground fifty yards away, the Colt still clutched in his left hand.

Then the square began to waver before his eyes and there was a terrible burning in his chest. Blinking, he looked down at himself and saw red blood spilling out between his clutching fingers. He tried to speak but he couldn't; his throat was clogged.

He looked up again dizzily and watched the wave of blackness rush at him across the square, break over him, followed by another and another.

That was when the buckboard reached the square. The woman in it dragged back the reins and braked suddenly, standing up. The people coming out from behind locked doors could see the look of stupefaction on her face. They watched how she half climbed, half fell from the buckboard and started walking across the square, then broke into a stiff, weaving run.

They saw too, the Reverend Bond's wife come rushing down St. Virgil Street with Louisa Harper. They watched the white-faced girl as she stood on the edge of the square, staring open-mouthed at the four figures on it. And they wondered.

He was still on his knees when Julia reached him. Both his arms were crossed tightly over his chest and stomach like those of a little boy who had eaten too many green apples and fallen sick. His blood was running over his arms and dripping on the ground.

She stood before her husband for several moments, one hand covering her lips, in her throat a sickened moaning as she looked down at him.

Abruptly, then, she gasped his name and fell to her knees beside him.

Slowly, in tiny, jerking movements, he raised his face to her. It was the face of a man who could not understand what had happened to him. For almost ten seconds, he stared at her, eyes dazed and unmoving, mouth hanging open.

Then, without a sound, he fell against her, dead.

She held his body in her arms, her face distorted by grief, dry sobs stabbing at her throat, hands stroking numbly at his back. She would remember for the rest of her life how it felt to have his warm blood running across her hands like water.

Fifty yards away, a father was leading his son, speaking to him in a stiff, proud voice.

"You're a brave boy," he said. "You did what had to be done. You're a very brave boy. We're all proud of you."

He failed to notice the look his son directed at him; one of sickened hatred and disgust.

He only became aware of what his son was feeling when Robby jerked his left arm free and staggered away, moving past Louisa without a word, his face a rigid mask of pain as he strode unevenly across the square.

It was three minutes after three P.M., September 14, 1879. The end of the third day.